ZAL AND ZARA AND
THE CHAMPIONS' RACE

Kit Downes was nineteen when he wrote his first book, *Zal and Zara and the Great Race of Azamed*. The idea of writing a story about the greatest magic carpet race in the world came to him in a café in Hay-on-Wye. He began the book the same day and finished it in his first term of university. He has now graduated and works as a teacher, spending his spare time travelling and searching for "good" stories as inspiration for his own writing. *Zal and Zara and the Champions' Race* is his second book.

First published 2012 by Walker Books Ltd
87 Vauxhall Walk, London SE11 5HJ

2 4 6 8 10 9 7 5 3 1

This book has been typeset in Goudy and Byron

Printed and bound in Great Britain by Clays Ltd, St Ives plc

British Library Cataloguing in Publication Data:
a catalogue record for this book is available from the British Library

ISBN 978-1-4063-0920-1

www.walker.co.uk

ZAL AND ZARA
AND THE
CHAMPIONS'
RACE

KIT DOWNES

**WALKER
BOOKS**

One

A sky of the brightest, palest blue imaginable vaulted over the Great Desert. Beneath it, the golden sands spread for thousands of miles in every direction, swept by the desert winds into crisp patterns of tall crests and rolling valleys. The sun stood high in the sky, a brilliant gold disc, shining down on Shirazar, the City of Butterflies, crown jewel of the Seventeen Kingdoms.

Shirazar was built on top of an enormous stone plateau. The ten-mile wide tabletop of sunset pink stone rose up out of the desert like an island from the sea. From somewhere far below it, water bubbled up through the plateau's natural tunnels and wells, feeding the city that was built over every inch of it. Shirazar was a rich garden city, its wealth shown by the golden domes and tall spires that filled its skyline. Every building was painted white to reflect the sun and in the morning light, the city streets shone like snow. In dozens of green parks and gardens, millions of butterflies, in every shade of every colour of the rainbow fluttered between fruit trees and flowers.

In the tallest spire of the Royal Palace, the ruler of Shirazar, Empress Haju, was holding her morning meeting with her ministers. Ten men were sitting around a long table, with the Empress' throne at the head. Built at the top of the spire, the council room did not have walls. Instead, tall windows overlooked the whole of Shirazar on every side, to remind everyone who governed there that their decisions reached far beyond the council room and so should always be made with compassion and justice. The First Minister of Shirazar, a tall man with a large moustache, was speaking.

"And so the crime wave finally seems to have come to an end, Your Majesty," he was saying. "There have been no more reported thefts or burglaries anywhere in the city since the Vessel of

Tears and the Mirror Curtain were stolen from the Shirazar Museum two weeks ago."

"Oh, good. That's a relief," said Empress Haju. "But are they any closer to catching them yet? Thieves on the loose are the last thing we need."

The Empress was young and beautiful, with creamy pale skin and curly chestnut hair. She was dressed in a long gown made of purple silk and decorated with peacock feathers. The silver crown of Shirazar sat neatly on her brow. The Empress was twenty-three and had come to the throne just two years ago, after her father – a fanatical butterfly collector – had run straight off the edge of the plateau while chasing a large and beautiful tiger moth. The Empress still wished, almost every day, that he had had the time to teach her just a little bit more about being an empress.

"I'm afraid not, Your Majesty," said the Second Minister of Shirazar. "I spoke to the captains of the Royal Protectors this morning. The thief, or thieves – whichever they may be – are extraordinarily good at not leaving any clues behind."

"Well, please tell the captains to redouble their efforts anyway," said the Empress. "Even if the crime wave seems to be over, we can't have wanted criminals running around the city during the Champions' Race."

The ministers all nodded. The Champions' Race was the pride and joy of Shirazar. It was held once every three years, when the finest flyers of all the Seventeen Kingdoms gathered in Shirazar to compete for the title of the greatest flyer in the Great Desert: the Champion of Champions. This would be the first race of Empress Haju's reign and she was determined that it should go well.

"On the subject of the Champions' Race, Your Majesty," said the Third Minister of Shirazar, "I have good news to report."

"Wait a minute!" said the Fourth Minister. "Is it the same news I've got?"

One of the pieces of advice Empress Haju's father had given her was never to have more than ten ministers to help her govern. This ensured that they were always overworked and therefore too busy to try anything underhand with their authority. It had the added advantage of discouraging anyone unscrupulous from applying for the job and brought to government only hard workers who thrived on pressure. The only problem was, the Empress reflected, that they always ended up competing with one another over everything, from who could be the most helpful to who could wear the largest turban and grow the longest moustache.

"How should I know if it's the same news you've got?" said the Third Minister, who was currently winning the largest turban competition. "What is it?"

The Fourth Minister leaned close and whispered it into his ear.

"Camelpat!" said the Third Minister. "Where did you hear it? When did you hear it?"

"Over breakfast this morning."

"Ha! Then I heard it first!" said the Third Minister. "Over dinner last night and from the man himself!" He turned back to the throne. "Paradim Nocturne is going to compete this year, Your Majesty."

"Oh!" The Empress sat up. "Really? The Red Squirrel is going to race again?"

Paradim Nocturne was the Champion of Shirazar, the reigning Champion of Champions, and possibly the greatest flyer who had ever lived. Flying under his nickname "the Red Squirrel" he had won the

9

Champions' Race an astonishing nineteen times in a row. The Empress had had a huge crush on him since she was thirteen.

"He's decided he wants to race one final time before he retires, Your Majesty," said the Fourth Minister.

"Didn't he say that last time?" said the Fifth Minister.

"Yes. And the time before that," said the Sixth Minister. "And the time before that."

"Even so, this is very good news," said the Empress. "Having Paradim involved should really help this race go well."

"Of course it will go well, Your Majesty. You're worrying unnecessarily," said the Seventh Minister. "The preparations are nearly complete. The race track has been marked out through the desert. The judges have been selected and they've agreed on this year's rule book. The extra seating for the spectators is under construction and we've even found some-one to sell discounted ice creams. Everything will be ready by the big day."

"The contestants are all here as well, Your Majesty," said the Eighth Minister. "The last team arrived yesterday: Zal Thesa and Zara Aura and their dog, Rip. The Champions of Azamed."

"Oh, I think I remember them," said the Empress. "Aren't they the ones who discovered how to weave flying carpets using all seven colours of magic six months ago?"

"Rediscovered, Your Majesty, yes," said the Ninth Minister. "In the Great Race of Azamed they left all the other contestants standing. It made all the international news scrolls. Now they're here to race with us."

"Oh, good," said the Empress. "More celebrities on the starting line can only be a good thing."

"You have nothing to worry about, Your Majesty," said the Tenth Minister. "You've thought of everything. There is nothing at all that could go wrong."

Above their heads, the ceiling of the council room had been painted with a beautiful fresco. It showed the Celestial Stork, the goddess of Shirazar and most of the other Seventeen Kingdoms, flying around the world through space, followed by her flock of children. The craftsmanship was exquisite. Real silver lined the birds' wings, diamonds were set into the ceiling to represent the stars and colourful gemstones marked the birds' eyes. If the Empress or any of her ministers had bothered to look up, they might have noticed that the eyes of the Stork of Fire had been carefully and silently removed. In their place, a pair of real eyes stared down into the room. The eyes were muddy brown and alive, flicking back and forth between the faces, following the conversation. At the mention of the Azamedian team and their magic carpet, the eyes blazed with a deep and burning fury.

"By all the Cosmos Vulture's tail feathers!"

In the tiny attic above the council room, a thin young man rose to his knees and angrily shoved the two large fire opals back into the Stork of Fire's eye sockets.

"Even here they're famous!"

He jumped to his feet and started to pace back and forth, grinding his fist into the palm of his hand. His movements made the candles flicker and his feet stirred up dust from the floor.

"Zal Thesa and Zara Aura! Everywhere I go, it's Zal Thesa and Zara Aura!"

The man was dressed entirely in brown. His

12

brown tunic was tucked into his brown trousers, which were tucked into brown socks inside brown shoes. He wore brown gloves and had a brown scarf wrapped entirely around his head, concealing all but his eyes. Around his neck he wore a bronze medallion on a long chain, carved with a symbol made of two elongated "S" shapes inside a circle. Pushed through his brown waist sash, he carried a large black dagger with a thick, wavy blade.

"Six months! Six months and they're still living on the glory of their supposed triumph!"

The young man was not alone in the attic. Sitting against one wall and watching him with respectful silence were two tall, muscular and dangerous-looking women and a young, nervous-looking boy. They all wore the same brown clothes, medallions and scarf-masks. Both the women wore long scimitars and the boy was clutching a crossbow.

"They'll pay! Oh, they'll pay! I swear, by all the Cosmos Vulture's dark and putrid toenails, they shall pay for every one of their crimes against me and my—!"

"Excuse me," said another voice. "Is this going anywhere?"

The man turned around. On the other side of the attic, sitting on an old crate and biting into a pear, was Sari Stormstrong. Sari was about twelve years old, though she did not know her own birthday and so could not be sure. She was a small, nimble girl, with the long, strong muscles of a rock climber. Her jet-black hair was pulled back into a long ponytail that hung down between her shoulders, apart from two strands that framed her face. Four long, thin, white scars, from an encounter with the claws of a hungry leopard, were drawn across her right cheek. She was dressed in a plain, rough woven tunic and trousers in rainforest green, with tough moccasins on her feet, and she watched the young man with her large, dark green eyes.

Sprawled on the floor around her were three full-grown tigers, two males and a female. The huge cats were lounging, resting their heads on their paws and lazily sweeping their tails back and forth across the floor. Their orange fur glowed in the candlelight as they looked on with big, yellow eyes.

"Of course it is, my dear," said the man, smiling behind his scarf. "Forgive me. I do have a tendency to ramble on. But you have no idea how much trouble those two have caused me."

The man was known as the Leader, though right at that moment, he was not the leader of very much. Six months ago, he had been the master of the Shadow Society, the secret organization founded in ancient times in Azamed by Salladan Shadow, magician, warrior, spy and prophet of the Cosmos Vulture. Over the centuries, the Society had grown into a vast and powerful crime syndicate, and the Leader had dreamed that under his leadership the Society would finally become powerful enough to overthrow the Caliph of Azamed and take over the city-kingdom. But that was before the Shadow Society's team – led by that almighty fool Haragan – had been caught cheating in the Great Race of Azamed. Afterwards, the Caliph – outraged at the Shadow Society's behaviour – had unleashed his guardsmen on them. In less time than the Leader had thought possible, the guards had dismantled every single part of his Society they could find. The rest of it had swiftly collapsed around him. With most of his men in jail, the Leader had had no choice but to flee Azamed, just hours after the race had ended. The only people he took with him were his two female bodyguards, Hara and Mira, and Etan, the sole member of Haragan's racing team who had managed to escape capture at the end of the race.

"You said you wanted to hire me, Mr Leader," Sari yawned. "Is there a job here or not? I've got other clients to see today."

"Yes, my dear, there is," said the Leader, rather frostily. "It's nothing complicated. Just something we won't have time to do ourselves. It should be child's play for someone like you. Etan?"

"Yes, sir!" Etan jumped to his feet and pulled out an old, yellowed scroll. He turned to Sari and then hesitated, looking at the tigers. Holding the scroll out at arm's length, he inched sideways across the room to hand it to her.

"You'll find that in room four hundred and seven, third floor, east wing of the Shirazar Museum," said the Leader, as Sari unrolled the scroll and Etan scurried back to his place. "Bring it to me intact and unopened. That's important. Five thousand gold pieces if you're successful."

"Twelve thousand," said Sari, studying the scroll.

"Six," said the Leader.

"Twelve."

"Seven."

"Twelve."

"Seven and a half!"

"Twelve," said Sari. "Or can't you afford it?"

"Mind your tongue, girl," said Hara. She and Mira rose to their feet, as smooth and graceful as panthers, placing their hands on their sword hilts. "If you want to keep it, that is."

"GGGGGGGRRRRRRRRRRRRRRRRRR!"

Teeth, claws and orange fur flashed across the room. Hara and Mira gasped as the tigers knocked them over backwards and pinned them to the floor with a thud that made the Empress and her ministers look up at the ceiling in the council room below.

"Vulture's beak!" yelled the Leader, jumping out of the way.

"Waaah!" Etan dropped his crossbow and scrambled backwards against the wall as the third tiger cornered him.

"Do you know how hard it'll be to break into the Shirazar Museum at the moment?" said Sari, who hadn't moved from her seat or looked up from the scroll. "They've got extra guards, better door locks and a whole new team of magicians."

"Yes," said the Leader. He straightened his clothes and composed himself. He stepped around the tiger holding Mira. "I'm aware security has been tightened since the Vessel of Tears and the Mirror Curtain were stolen two weeks ago. But I'm surprised that it matters. You see, I thought you were meant to be Sari Stormstrong."

He folded his arms and looked Sari in the eye before continuing.

"I thought you were the only person ever to break into the Impenetrable Vault of the Imperial Bank of Pursolon. I thought you raided the Royal Tombs of Hothath and stripped a hundred dead kings of their burial treasure. I thought you were the one who stole the Diamond Crown of Endsali, right out of the throne room, and the Rajah of Gothopar's moustache – literally from under his nose. I thought you were meant to be the greatest thief in the Seventeen Kingdoms."

"I am," said Sari, with a smile, "so I'm also the most expensive."

"Eight thousand," said the Leader.

"Twelve," said Sari. "If you want someone cheaper, Mr Leader, go and find them. Someone who'd do it for five thousand might even make it over the museum's garden wall before they get caught. But if you actually want this," she held up the scroll, "it's going to cost you twelve thousand."

There was a long pause. Hara and Mira watched from under the tigers.

"All right! Fine!" said the Leader. "Twelve thousand it is. But only when you bring it to me! You're not seeing a single coin in advance, young lady! And don't expect me to pay for expenses!"

"Sure. We have a deal," said Sari. She rolled up the scroll and stood up. "Come on, Sheertooth, Cloudclaw, Jeweltail. Time to go."

The three tigers crept backwards, releasing the Shadows, and followed Sari towards the door.

"Excuse me!" said the Leader, who had expected to spend at least an hour telling Sari exactly how he wanted her to carry out the theft. "Where are you going?"

"I told you. I've got another client to see today," said Sari. "Don't worry, Mr Leader. You'll get your box."

"It's not a box! It's a... Never mind," said the Leader. "But I'd better get it! Don't even think of coming to find me without it, young lady! I've got no guarantee you can do this, after all!"

"Oh, I can," said Sari. She looked back and smiled. "Who do you think broke into the museum two weeks ago to steal the Vessel of Tears and the Mirror Curtain?"

Two

Not far from the palace, songbirds chirped and twit-
tered in the gardens of the Imperial Hotel. The
garden was a long green rectangle, with a trimmed
lawn, several fountains and a large stone patio. At
the far end was a small apple orchard, of just six
trees. Under the shade of their leafy branches, Zal
Thesa was practising.

He was standing in the middle of the orchard, in
front of a tall wooden stepladder he had borrowed
from the hotel's caretakers. His small, dark-furred
dog Rip was standing on top of it, along with a
small pile of fallen apples they had collected from
around the roots of the trees. Zal was twelve years
old, though his thirteenth birthday was not far

away. He was a short, thin and handsome boy, with the slender, muscular build that came from long hours of sword-fencing practice. His light brown hair was swept forwards and upwards into a crest, in an attempt to keep it out of his eyes. Tucked into his red waist sash was a long, light scimitar, with a slender moon-curved blade hidden inside its black scabbard. The wooden grip of the hilt was worn into grooves the shape of Zal's fingers.

Zal stood with his feet apart and relaxed, feeling all the tension sink out of his body. Rip watched from the top of the ladder. Zal stared straight ahead and concentrated on letting his mind go blank, blocking out distractions and clearing away all his thoughts, especially questions and doubts. Only one thing mattered now. That was speed.

"OK, boy," Zal said. "Now."

Rip lowered his nose and pushed one of the apples off the top of the ladder. It dropped straight down into Zal's field of vision. The muscles in his sword arm exploded. Zal's right hand shot across his body. His fingers closed around his sword hilt, instantly finding the perfect grip. Zal turned his left shoulder forwards and his right one backwards, whipping his sword out of its scabbard and upwards across his body in a perfect, lightning-fast diagonal-draw-cut. The steel blade sang as it left the scabbard, flew through the air and sliced effortlessly through the apple, sending the two halves flying in opposite directions. Zal stopped his arm dead, holding his sword as still as a pool of water in a cave deep inside a mountain. The two halves of the apple landed with the halves of all the others he had practised with, in two small piles on opposite sides of the orchard.

"Camelpat!" Zal stepped back and lowered his sword. It still was not right.

"Wraff, waff," said Rip, from the top of the ladder.

Zal nodded. He was getting better. His drawing technique was fine and his accuracy was perfect. But he still was not fast enough. And he needed to be faster than fast when he was facing *him*. Zal slid his sword back into his scabbard. He spread his feet a little further apart on the grass, and tried again.

"Zal? Where are you?"

"AAAAHH!"

Zal jumped and his sword sunk into the wooden leg of the stepladder.

"WRAFF!" cried Rip, as the ladder toppled over,

23

tipping him and the apples onto the grass and pulling Zal's sword out of his hand.

"ZARA!"

"What?" said Zara Aura, as she stepped into the orchard and looked at Zal, who was wrestling to pull his sword out of the ladder's leg while Rip dug himself out of the apples. "What are you doing?"

Zara was a small, slim and pretty girl, with green eyes and blonde hair that just touched the bottoms of her ears. She was the same age as Zal, but a few centimetres shorter. As well as being one of the Champions of Azamed, she was a senior student at the school run by Azamed's Guild of Magicians. She was also Zal's best friend, his former worst enemy, his carpet-racing and carpet-weaving partner and – reluctantly – his fiancée.

"Practising!" said Zal, as he pulled his sword out of the ladder. Thankfully, the blade wasn't chipped. "You just—"

"Well, stop. It's time for breakfast," said Zara. "Come on. I want to go out."

Zal rolled his eyes, but sheathed his sword and followed her up the garden to the hotel. It was a tall white building with fifteen floors and lots of balconies. They went across the patio and into their ground floor suite, brushing aside the muslin curtain that hung across the open doors. The suite was bright and airy, with high white walls and soft, fluffy carpets on the floor. Large sofas and armchairs were set in a square in one half of the main room and in the other stood a wooden dining table, spread with the hotel's extravagant complimentary breakfast. Zara's father, Arna Aura, was already sitting at it.

"Gwwd mwrning, Zwl!" he said, through a large mouthful. "Cwme wnd swt dwn. It's gwing fwst."

"Thanks, Mr Aura," said Zal, as Rip scampered over to the hotel's extra-large complimentary dog-food bowl. "So where do you want to go?" he said to Zara.

"Where do you think?" said Zara. She sat down and unrolled a tourist scroll. "We're in Shirazar. I want to go to the Royal Palace and the Magician's Academy and the Library of Magic and the Tomb of Heroes and the Butterfly Bridge and the Sunset Caves and the Statue Gardens. This morning, anyway. This afternoon, I want to go to—"

"Hold on," said Zal. "I've been to all of those before."

25

Now that he had sat down, Zal realized he wasn't hungry. He got up and went over to the suite's full-length mirror. He placed his hand on his sword hilt and relaxed again.

"You have, but I haven't," said Zara. "This is my first trip to Shirazar, remember? I want to see everything."

"Mmm! And you're never going to forget it," said Arna, pausing in refilling his plate. Zara's father was a large man with a short beard and a huge stomach. "Shirazar is the shining emerald of the Great Desert. There are mysteries and wonders to be found here around every corner. It's one of the greatest cities of the Seventeen Kingdoms. Second only to dear old Azamed, eh, Augur?"

"Mmm? Oh, yes. Absolutely."

The voice came from the other side of a giant block of magic carpets that stood in the middle of the room. They were rolled up and fastened with string, then stacked like logs and tied together in a big rectangular block, six across and eight high. They were all brand new seven-coloured rainbow carpets that Zal had woven and Zara had enchanted. Zal's father, Augur Thesa, peered over the top of them. He was a tall, thin man with a long beard that hung down to his waist. Azamedian flying carpets were popular in Shirazar and Augur and Arna – who were both friends and business partners – had brought forty-eight of Zal and Zara's finest ones to sell to the city's many magic carpet shops. Augur was going over each one, checking against a long list to make sure it had survived the trip from Azamed undamaged.

"It's a splendid city," he said. "Why did you never come with us before, Zara?"

"Because she always had magic contests to go to," said Zal, who was staring at himself in the mirror. He whipped out his sword again, in another fast diagonal-draw-cut, aiming at his reflection's neck. He stopped the sword just before it touched the glass.

"They were important," said Zara. "But I'm here now and I want to see Shirazar. You don't have to come."

"That's not what I meant," said Zal. "This isn't a holiday. We're here to race. We need to start training."

"Now, now. There's five days to go until the

race," said Augur. "There'll be plenty of time for practising after Zara's done some sightseeing."

"No, there won't," said Zal, looking at his father in the mirror. "This isn't like racing at home. This is the Champions' Race. We're up against the finest flyers in the Seventeen Kingdoms. They're going to be out training already."

"Bwfwre brwkfwst?" said Arna.

"Why are you so worried?" said Zara. "You never used to get this excited about races."

"Are you crazy?" said Zal, looking over his shoulder. "This might be our last chance to race on the Rainbow Carpet."

It was true that he never used to be interested – at all – in magic carpets or racing on them. Zal's ambition was to join the Caliph's Guard, the fearless soldiers and policemen who patrolled the streets of Azamed, protecting the city from danger. But that was before the Shadow Society had set fire to his father's carpet shop, trying to win the Great Race before it had begun. It was before Zara had led him on an astonishing adventure around Azamed and back into the mists of his city's past, where they had learnt the real history of magic carpets. It was before he had woven the first seven-colour carpet in centuries, the Rainbow Carpet that many said was impossible, and before he and Zara had ridden it to a glorious victory in the Great Race. The moment they crossed the finishing line, flying through applause and flower blossoms, Zal realized he had fallen in love with magic carpets.

Unfortunately, his chances of racing on the Rainbow Carpet again were slim. The seven-colour carpet had turned out to be so fast that the Caliph of Azamed had declared it definitely gave them an unfair advantage. He had decreed that in the future, only six-colour carpets or less would be allowed to compete in the Great Race. But as Zal and Zara were the clear winners – and had overcome the Shadow Society team's determined cheating – he recognized them as Azamed's new champions, and announced that they would be allowed to represent their city in the Champions' Race, using the Rainbow Carpet.

"Unless we win the Champions' Race and we can defend the title next year, that's it," said Zal. "We'll never get to race on the Rainbow Carpet again. At least not until we've sold enough to hold a rainbow carpet race. But that won't be the same."

"Zal, I'm delighted!" said Augur. "You've finally learnt how special magic carpets are."

"Cwrtwnly!" said Arna. "And just think, if you do win, we'll be almost sure to get the Carpet Seller of the Year Award."

Even though seven-colour carpets had been banned from the Great Race, Augur's carpet shop in Azamed was overflowing with orders for them. Even if they could never race on them, many people still wanted to own a rainbow carpet of the kind that was mentioned so often in Azamed's legends. Some people were already talking of organizing a new race just for rainbow carpets, where piloting skill would be tested much more than speed. As only Augur and Arna and their children knew the secret to weaving rainbow carpets – and they were determined to take it to their graves – the two fathers were making a fortune out of selling their new rainbow carpets and were well on the way to becoming the richest carpet sellers in Azamed.

"Well, I want to race on it again too," said Zara, as Zal made yet another diagonal-draw-cut. "But I want to see the city as well and … and… What are you doing?"

"Practising," said Zal.

"How's that going to help with the race?"

"Not for the race! He's going to be here any minute."

"Who?"

There were three short, jaunty knocks on the hotel suite door.

"Aha!"

Zal spun around and sheathed his sword. He quickly smoothed the creases out of his tunic, then ran to the door and flung it open, throwing his arms wide and smiling.

"MILES!" he cried.

"ZAL!" cried the boy who was standing in the hall in the same position, arms thrown wide and with a beaming smile on his face. He was also wearing a sword.

They stayed like that for just an instant. Then their eyes turned to steel. Zal and the boy's hands shot across their bodies and grabbed their sword hilts. The metal rang as they ripped them from their scabbards and launched twin, lightning fast diagonal-draw-cuts, aiming at each other's necks.

CLAAANG!!!

Zara squeezed her eyes shut as the two blades collided and locked together. Zal and the boy were frozen in place. Zal's blade was stuck, halfway to the target, locked against the boy's sword hilt. The boy's blade had made it all the way and was just touching the side of Zal's neck.

"Ha!" cried the boy, jumping back. "Still slow!"

"Camelpat!" said Zal, lowering his sword. "How do you do it?!"

"It's all in the feet. Just like I always tell you," said the boy. "And it's great to see you, by the way."

"Yes, it really is," said Zal. "Miles!"

"Zal!"

They threw out their arms again, stepped forward and hugged each other, being careful to keep their swords out of the way.

"Miles, my boy!" said Arna, striding around the table. "How wonderful to see you! But where the Stork is your father?"

"Hi, Mr Aura. Great to see you too," said the boy, shaking Arna's hand. He was about the same height as Zal, with thick, curly red hair, blue-grey eyes and an open, friendly face. "Dad says sorry. He and Celeste are out training. But you're all invited

32

to lunch tomorrow. Hello, Rip!"

"Wraff, wraff!" Rip dashed over to the door and jumped around Miles' feet until he squatted down to scratch the dog between his ears.

"Meow!"

At that moment, a large, fluffy Pursolonian cat, with pale blue eyes and thick, snow-white fur, looked around the door.

"WRAFF!" barked Rip.

"MEOW!" said the cat, all its fur standing up on end.

Rip and the cat launched themselves at each other. They collided in the air and locked together into a single furry black-and-white ball. They rolled, biting and scratching, across the carpet.

"Hello, Fluffy," said Zal, stepping out of the way.

"Some things never change," said Augur, smiling and shaking his head. "Hello, Miles."

"Hello, Mr Thesa."

"Shouldn't we stop them?" said Zara, as the two pets bounced, hissing and barking, off one of the sofas.

"Oh, don't worry. They're always like this," said Miles, just as the cat and dog came to a stop on one of the rugs. Rip lay panting, with Fluffy half on top and half underneath him, and then started licking Fluffy's head. She purred happily.

"Zara, this is Miles Nocturne," said Arna. "The son of an old and dear friend from our past visits to Shirazar. He and Zal used to train at the School of Swords together."

"Oh, how do you do?" said Zara, shaking his hand.

"Very well, thanks, Zara. It's great to meet you at last," said Miles. "Zal's been complaining about you for years."

"Shut up, Miles," said Zal.

"Oh, really?" said Zara. Then she blinked, looking at Miles. "Wait … Nocturne? Not as in…"

"Yes. As in Paradim Nocturne," said Arna, clapping Miles on the shoulder. "This is the Red Squirrel's son."

"Wait a minute!" said Zal, spinning around. "Did you say out training? You don't mean…"

"Yes. That's what I came to tell you," said Miles. "Dad's decided he's going to compete this year."

Despite its immense beauty, the Great Desert was a harsh and hostile place to live. The civilizations that had grown up in it or around its edges had all learnt early in their history that the safest, most convenient way to travel across the burning wastes was to fly.

Each kingdom had developed its own means for doing this, either by capturing and taming the giant flying animals that had evolved in the Great Desert, or by learning to infuse flying magic into various objects. All of the kingdoms had done this, except for Shirazar.

It was not from lack of trying. Shirazar's magicians had worked tirelessly for centuries, trying to create flying objects. Explorers and adventurers had searched the furthest corners of the continent, looking for new flying animals. But somehow they were never successful. Shirazar remained the only kingdom with its feet stuck firmly on the ground.

To begin with, this had not posed a major problem. Shirazar was wealthy enough from trade that its citizens could easily buy any means of flight they chose from the other kingdoms. But over the centuries, as each of the other kingdoms' unique means of flight became an important part of its culture, Shirazar began to feel ashamed of being the odd kingdom out. Its failure to find its own means of flight became a source of great sadness for the city and its people.

Five hundred years ago, Empress Haju's ancestor, Emperor Clearju, had decided to do something about it. Studying the other kingdoms, he realized they all had one thing in common: every year, they each held some sort of ultimate flying race, to establish who was the greatest flyer in their kingdom. There was the Royal Aerial Regatta of Pursolon, the Air Contest of the Heaven Steppe, the Wind Chase of the Silk Lands and the Great Race of Azamed. Why shouldn't there be, the Emperor mused, some sort of international race, where the winners of these races could compete against each other to determine who was the greatest flyer in the Great Desert? And Shirazar, with no means of flight of its own, would be the perfect, neutral place to hold it.

The Emperor wrote immediately to the rulers of the other kingdoms explaining his idea and they all responded with enthusiasm. The other kingdoms had often held small, local competitions with their nearest neighbours, racing two means of flight against each other, but no one had thought of bringing all sixteen champions together before. They immediately dispatched their current title-holders to Shirazar to compete in the first ever, hastily named "Champion Flyer of the Great Desert" race.

It was a tremendous success. Despite the Champions of Katrasca's dramatic crash and the Champions of Quakajak trying to eat the other contestants because they had misunderstood part of the rule book, the race was a triumph. Racing the different means of flight against each other turned out to be far more exciting than anyone had imagined. During the Champion of Xalam's victory party, the ambassadors of all the other kingdoms publicly called on the Emperor to make the race a regular event and he agreed.

The celebrations in Shirazar lasted for a month. The kingdom had finally found its place among the flying kingdoms. But the happiness was tinged with sadness because even though they were now hosting the ultimate flying race, no Shirazan would ever be able to compete in it.

Forty years ago, a boy had been born in Shirazar who would change that. His name was Paradim Nocturne and he first watched the Champions' Race when he was seven, sitting on his father's shoulders. It was the most thrilling thing he had ever seen. As soon as the winner crossed the finish line and the cheering died down, Paradim announced to his parents that he would fly in the race when he grew up. His parents smiled sadly and explained why that was impossible.

But Paradim was not discouraged. He listened to his parents, but told them that, nevertheless, he would compete in the Champions' Race one day. He also told his friends, his relatives, his school teachers, the customers in his mother and father's shop and anyone he happened to meet in the street. Once they had finished laughing and realized he was serious, they asked how he thought he was going to do it.

Paradim applied himself to the problem. For five years, he studied the history of the Champions' Race and of Shirazar's search for its own means of flight. As he was not a magician, he studied alchemy and potion-making. Some of the formulas he made were impressive for a self-taught twelve-year-old working in his bedroom but, unfortunately, none of them worked. Nothing he painted over the legs of his bed made it fly, nothing he fed to his mother's pet water dragons made them grow wings and nothing he did to any of the butterflies he caught with his friend, Empress Haju's father, then the Crown Prince of Shirazar, caused them to grow big enough to ride on. Paradim eventually reasoned that only a true magician, born with the Gift to control the seven shades of magic, would be able to create a means of flight by magic.

Paradim tried a different course. He consulted magicians, mystics and astrologers. He meditated for hours, trying to fly by willpower alone. He visited the local temple and prayed to the Celestial Stork, asking her to send him a sign. Finally, one night after his fifteenth birthday, Paradim had a dream. In it, he was floating among purple clouds. Suddenly, the clouds were swept aside and out of them flew a giant stork, with a man riding on its back. The man had a long red ponytail that was streaming out behind him in the wind.

The following morning, Paradim packed a bag and ran away from home. He hitched a ride on a trading caravan and headed out into the Great Desert. For the next year, he searched for the meaning of his dream. He trekked through the peaks of Tabaras and the mountains of the Heaven Steppe. He explored the jungles of Gothopar and Quakajak. He sailed along the coast of Endsali and through the islands of the Emerald Archipelago, before finally arriving on the icy plains of Frostbite.

The northernmost kingdom was made of snow-fields, glaciers and mountains of stone and ice. Paradim was not expecting to find much there, but after trudging for three days across the snowy plains, he found a lake, which was fed by warm water from an underground volcano and never froze.

It was later named Stork Lake. The first thing Paradim saw as he climbed over the last snow drift was a huge cloud of storks, taking off from the lake's water and flapping into the air. Paradim thought it was strange to find so many storks there. There were no plants or trees around the lake and the waters were so warm that there were not many fish. So why did so many storks come there?

Paradim spent three months living by the lake. At night, he shivered in his tent inside two sleeping bags. During the day he competed with the storks to catch fish and shellfish, and searched around the lake for an answer. On the last day of the third month, when Paradim was cold, hungry and more than ready to give up and go home, he found the mouth of a cave, leading deep into the ice that lay under the snow.

It was just large enough for him to crawl down. The tunnel ran through the snow and ice and into the frozen soil of Frostbite below it. Paradim could not see his hand in front of his face in the darkness and the tunnel was so long that crawling through it took hours. Finally, it widened and Paradim found by touch that it had ended in a small round chamber. In the middle, his hands found a nest made of dried weeds, which must have been carried up from the bottom of the lake. Inside it lay the smooth, round shape of a giant frozen egg.

It was big enough that Paradim had to carry it in both his arms. With just enough room to turn around in the chamber, he crawled back to the surface. He placed the egg in a crevice in the rocks and sat down to watch as the sun melted the frost from its shell.

For the next three days, Paradim focused all his attention on the egg. During the day, he carried it around the lake, keeping it in the warmest patches of sunlight he could find. At night, he wrapped it in his spare socks and built a large fire to keep it warm. Finally, on the morning of the third day, Paradim was woken by the sound of the egg cracking. He watched in amazement as a huge, fluffy stork chick emerged, blinking in the sunlight. Paradim immediately tried to feed it and it pecked his fingers. But still, he went down on his knees and – with the chick watching curiously – prayed his thanks to the Celestial Stork.

Paradim spent a year at the lake, raising the chick himself. He named her Celeste, in gratitude to the Celestial Stork for sending her to him. She had hatched as large as a normal adult stork and Paradim hunted for hours to keep her well fed. To his surprise, the other storks at the lake helped him, bringing Celeste the biggest and tastiest fish from the lake's depths. Celeste grew very quickly. By the time she was three months old, Paradim stopped using his tent and started sleeping under one of her wings, which was more comfortable and much warmer. By six months, Celeste had grown as large as a Heaven Steppe dragon. Her wingspan stretched ten metres and her beak was as long as a spear. Paradim had to climb up her legs, which were as thick as trees, to get onto her back and together, with help from the other storks, they learnt how to fly.

After a year, Paradim packed his rucksack and said goodbye to the storks at the lake and he and Celeste flew south towards Shirazar. It had taken him a full year to travel overland to the lake, but Celeste made the trip in six days. They arrived in Shirazar just as the contestants were arriving for that year's Champions' Race.

Paradim's arrival caused quite a stir. After going straight home to see his parents – who were both delighted and furious to see him – Paradim flew to the Royal Palace, where Empress Haju's father, recently crowned as Emperor, was holding lunch for the newly arrived Champions.

The Emperor almost choked on a camel kebab when he saw the giant stork landing in his gardens and scaring his prized butterflies. He was even more surprised when a strange, long-haired teenager jumped down from its back and ran over to introduce himself as his old friend, Paradim Nocturne. Paradim apologized for the interruption, explained where he had found Celeste, how he had learnt to fly on her and asked to represent Shirazar in the Champions' Race.

At first, the Emperor was reluctant to agree. Like all Shirazans, he had dreamed of competing in the race himself. But he was worried that if he agreed it would alter Shirazar's neutral status as the host of the Champions' Race. Then to his surprise, the other contestants came to his rescue and asked that Paradim and Celeste be allowed to compete. They were all Champions, but none of them had ever matched wings with a giant stork before. All of them were keen to see if their means of flight could beat Celeste. The Emperor agreed, but on one condition. Paradim could fly in the race, but as he had never competed before, he would not be given the title of Champion of Shirazar. He would only get that if he won.

Paradim and Celeste had five days to prepare. They trained hard for the first three days and then rested for the last two. Shirazar's magicians and natural historians came to examine Celeste and were amazed by her. From what Paradim told them, they could only conclude that she must be the last

of an extinct species of ancient stork and her egg
must have been preserved by the underground ice
in Frostbite, probably for centuries. Amongst the
people of Shirazar, excitement was at a fever pitch.
Could she win the Champions' Race?

On the morning of the race, Paradim was nervous,
sensing that his whole kingdom's hopes were riding
on his shoulders. While he was getting ready in
his bedroom, he absent-mindedly noticed that his
red hair had grown very long while he had been
at the lake and now hung halfway down his back.
Remembering how during the trip back to Shirazar
he had constantly had to brush it out of his eyes,
Paradim tied it back in a ponytail and then went to
get Celeste.

An hour later, they were on the starting line. As
Paradim tried to hide his trembling from the other
contestants, who were all much more experienced,
he heard thousands of Shirazans chanting his name.
But then, Paradim caught a glimpse of his reflection
in one of the bronze shields mounted on the vimana
of the Gothopar team. He was sitting on the back of
a giant stork and the desert wind was lifting his long
red ponytail behind him. In the seconds before the

race started, Paradim realized he had turned into the man in his almost-forgotten dream. His nervousness disappeared. The race began and he and Celeste launched over the starting line towards their destiny. Half an hour later, they crossed the finishing line in first place. They had kept on winning ever since.

"He is racing again?" said Zal. "Oh, great! We're finished!"

"Sorry to be the bearer of bad news," said Miles.

"Wasn't he retiring last time?" said Zara. "He's won nineteen times already."

"He wants to make it twenty before he retires," said Miles. "You know what Dad's like, Zal. He's a bit superstitious. He thinks it would be bad luck to retire on an odd number."

"We're finished!" said Zal, again. "We'll never get to race the Rainbow Carpet again! He'll beat us, and then we won't have a chance to defend the title next year! We haven't even got to the starting line, and we've already—"

"Zal, get a grip!" said Arna. "The race hasn't started yet. It most certainly hasn't finished."

"Quite right," said Augur. "Paradim may be a formidable opponent, but he's never faced a rainbow carpet before. None of the Champions have."

"Are these them?" said Miles. He went over to the block of rainbow carpets and walked around it. Fluffy sniffed at them and mewed with interest. "Which one is it?"

"None of them," said Zara. "Those are just the ones we brought to sell. This is it."

She went to the corner of the room, where another rolled-up carpet was standing on its end against the wall. Everyone stopped and watched as Zara lowered it to the floor and unrolled it.

The Rainbow Carpet – the first one she and Zal had woven and enchanted together – unfurled across the floor. The seven colours glowed in the light coming through the windows. Magic sparkled among the threads like diamonds. White doves, water dragons and the crown of an ancient emperor decorated its corners and edges. Zara touched it with her hand, feeling her magic flow down her arm and mix with the magic in the carpet. The carpet rose up off the floor and floated, perfectly still and even, shining like a rectangle cut from a rainbow.

"Wow!" said Miles, gazing at it with wide eyes.

"Can Celeste do that?" said Zal. "Seriously. Can she?"

Rip hopped onto the carpet and gave a sharp bark. Fluffy sniffed at it cautiously, and then sprang up beside him.

"Perhaps you should go out for some practice," said Augur, as Arna pushed the window-doors open all the way.

"Yes," said Zara.

"Let's," said Zal. "Come on, Miles."

"Really?" said Miles. "It's OK for me to—"

"Come on," said Zara, sitting down in the pilot's position. Rip sat beside her, wagging his tail. Zal sat down on the tail end of the carpet, with Miles in the middle holding Fluffy. Zara pressed both her hands on the soft pile of the carpet, feeling the connection with the magic once again. She pushed, half with her hands and half with her magic and the carpet turned around elegantly to face the open window-doors.

"Hold tight," said Zal.

"Please," said Miles. "I've been taking rides on Celeste since I was… WHOOOOOOAAA!"

The carpet leapt forwards like an arrow from a

bow. They shot through the window-doors and out into the golden sunlight. Zara leant backwards, pulling the front of the carpet up as they zoomed down the garden, sending the butterflies spinning out of their way, and rose up over the apple orchard, their slipstream ripping leaves off the trees. The ground fell away beneath them as they climbed high up over the streets of the city. Fluffy mewed and Rip barked as they levelled out and flew forwards at full speed above the rooftops and gardens, weaving between golden domes and tall spires.

"HOLY STORK!" shouted Miles, over the wind, which was blowing his curly hair almost straight.

"What do you think?" Zal shouted, smiling. Up ahead he could see Shirazar, stretching away to the edge of the plateau. The vast blue sky and the golden sands of the desert, where they would be racing in five days time, lay beyond.

"What do I…? Holy Stork!" gasped Miles. "I think the race is going to be exciting this year!"

Three

Night had fallen and Shirazar lay sleeping beneath a deep black sky, lightly dusted with stars. A crescent moon looked down on the closed shops and empty streets. In front of the Shirazar Museum, a lone guard was patrolling beside the garden wall. White-winged moon butterflies fluttered like ghosts across the lawns. Fireflies glowed among the blades of grass. Apart from the clank of the guard's armour, everything was silent.

A dart, made from a needle of bone fletched with crimson parrot feathers, flew through a crack in the wall with a whispering hiss and struck the guard in the neck. The guard opened his mouth to shout out, but the Sleeping Snake venom worked too quickly.

His spear fell from his hand and the guard crumpled onto the grass and was soon snoring.

Two slim hands gripped the top of the wall. A second later, Sari peeped over the top, a bamboo blowpipe held between her teeth. She looked quickly in both directions. There were no more guards in sight. Perfect.

Sari pulled herself up and rolled over the top of the wall, landing as lightly as a cat on the other side. She had switched her green tunic and trousers for a black outfit and she wore a black handkerchief tied over the lower half of her face. Around her waist was a belt laden with small pouches, containing all the tools she needed for tonight's job.

On the other side of the wall, claws scraped against the stone. Three orange tails flashed in the moonlight as Sheertooth, Cloudclaw and Jeweltail jumped over the wall and landed beside Sari with soft thumps. Sari placed her hands on her tigers' flanks, feeling their hearts beating beneath their warm fur. They were hiding it well. But underneath, they were just as excited as she was.

Between them and the museum was a long flowerbed, blocking their way to the lawn. It was filled with red, yellow and orange flowers. Sari stopped and stared at them. She frowned. There was something strange about them. Even in the moonlight, their colours were bright and garish. Beneath them, stems and vines covered with thorns coiled across the soil like snakes. Jeweltail sniffed at the edge of the flowerbed and growled. Sari nodded, reached into one of her belt pouches and drew out a small handful of dried meat pieces. She stood up and threw them over the flowerbed, flicking her wrist so they spread out through the air. Instantly, several of the flowers snapped shut, snatching the pieces of meat out of the air. The closed blossoms writhed and rippled with a soft chewing sound. When they opened again, there was no trace of the meat left inside them. Sari snorted. As if *that* was really going to stop anyone. And even if it did, there was nothing – and no one – that could stop *her*.

Cloudclaw purred at the challenge. He backed up to the wall, took a running jump and sailed over the flowerbed. Several flowers snapped shut beneath him as he landed safely on the far side. He looked around and growled with triumph. Sheertooth and Jeweltail rolled their eyes but followed him across.

Sari, who could not jump that far, dashed along to an apple tree that grew beside the wall and swarmed up its trunk and into its branches. She had been taught to climb by monkeys and even in the dark her hands and feet found branches and footholds easily. She stretched for the longest branch which reached the furthest over the flowerbed, crawled along it and hung beneath it like a sloth, swung herself back and forwards twice and let go. She did a double-forwards-somersault through the air, her black ponytail flying behind her, and landed safely on the edge of the flowerbed. Two blossoms snapped shut behind her heels. The tigers growled. Sari rubbed their heads, and together they ran silently across the lawn towards the museum. The white-winged moon butterflies fluttered out of their way and fireflies were crushed beneath their shoes and paws.

The locks on the ground floor windows had been replaced with better ones since she was last here two weeks ago. The new ones were triple-levered and quadruple-sprung, sensitive enough to resist any lock pick. Assuming that was, that the lock pick was made of metal. Sari reached into her belt pouch and pulled out a long white swan feather. She slipped it into the lock and twirled it gently back and forth, until the lock clicked open. Sari slid the window up and for the second time, they entered the museum.

The corridor was long and empty. Even Sari's breathing seemed to echo off the tall white walls as she slipped over the windowsill and lowered her feet to the polished floor. Sheertooth followed behind her and then froze. His ears twitched. He put his head down low and raised his hackles. Sari listened and heard it too, paws thundering softly against the floor and tails swishing in the dark. The sound grew closer as Jeweltail and Cloudclaw climbed in through the window, until five jet-black guard dogs ran around the corner ahead of them, teeth bared and tongues lolling, their eyes burning for their prey. They took one look at the tigers and stopped in their tracks. Their eyes went wide and they turned and ran straight back the way they had come, yelping with terror. They fled straight into the nearest exhibit room and hid whimpering under the biggest display table. Sari smiled. Obviously, the dogs remembered them from their last visit. She led the way towards the stairs.

They saw no other dogs or guards as they hurried up to the third floor. The enormous museum was dedicated to the entire history of Shirazar and the Great Desert. The rooms and exhibition halls contained statues, pots, paintings, weapons, ancient means of flight, suits of armour, dinosaur skeletons, gold and silver jewellery, diamonds and other treasures. Many of the exhibits were worth small fortunes, but Sari ignored them. She was a professional and she only stole what she was being paid – and paid well – to steal.

They rounded a corner near room four hundred and seven and stopped dead in the face of a dazzling gold light. The tigers growled and blinked. Sari threw up a hand to shield her eyes. She squinted through her fingers. Very clever. The otherwise empty corridor was protected by a casting lantern. The glass and bronze lamp hung from the ceiling ahead of them and the magic flame inside it filled the corridor with golden light. If a casting lantern cast a shadow, the small bronze bell that was hanging beneath it would immediately begin to ring, summoning every guard in the wing. But a shadow was just a place where there was no light.

Sari felt in her belt pouches and drew out her sun crystal. Forged by tremendous heat in the depths of space long ago, it was a large, diamond-shaped stone, with edges so sharp that they almost cut her palm. It had fallen to earth fused inside a meteorite and she had bought it for thirty gold pieces from a disreputable amulet trader at a smugglers' market in the Deep Desert and, so far, it had been worth every coin. Sari closed her eyes and held the crystal behind her back. She rubbed it against her sleeve and a tiny speck of light started to glow within it. As she continued to rub it, the speck grew, becoming brighter and brighter. The tigers shut their eyes. The light became an intense golden blaze, equal to the light of the sun, illuminating the dark corridor behind them as bright as the desert at midday. Sari walked forward into the casting lantern's light. The lantern cast her shadow and the light of the sun crystal instantly filled it up again. The bell trembled, but did not start ringing. Sari and the tigers walked straight under the lantern, and out of its reach, and through the door of room four hundred and seven.

Inside, the room was filled with a neatly organized collection of different artefacts. Tools, weapons, pot shards, broken statues, paintings, models, toys and kitchen utensils lay in display cases or were mounted on the walls around the room. According to the exhibit sign they all came from somewhere called Jaktivar, which Sari had never heard of. But that did not matter, as she quickly saw the item they had come for, sitting on a table in the middle of the room.

The sand-coloured box was an almost perfect cube, half a metre long on each side. It was made of stone and its sides were scratched and scarred, its edges and corners chipped. Four deep grooves, carved close together, ran around all four sides of it. The lid fitted into the top so tightly that there was only a hair-thin crack to show it was there, with some writing in an alphabet Sari could not read carved across it. The wooden table where it sat was highly polished and surrounded by a red velvet rope, held up on four metal stands.

Sari reached over the rope and placed both her hands on the box. She pushed gently across the table top to test its weight. The box wobbled, and so did the table. Sari paused and looked down. The table was not actually resting on the floor. There were two centimetres of space between the granite flagstones and the table's legs. The table was floating in the air. Sari let go of the box and touched the table and felt it pushing upwards against her hand, like a magnet repelling another one away. She smiled. A levitation spell. The table had been enchanted to fly. Without the weight of the box holding it down, it would go straight up towards the ceiling, where there hung another bronze bell, ready to ring and summon the guards.

"Sheer," whispered Sari.

Sheertooth stood up and placed both his heavy paws on the table. Sari lifted the box off. The table buckled as it tried to rise, but Sheertooth held it steady. Sari set the box down on the floor, still inside the velvet rope, and gripped the edge of the table. She nodded to Sheertooth and counted silently to three. Sheer pulled his paws off. As the table shot up, Sari flipped it over. It flew straight downwards with some force and Sari just had time to grab its legs and stop it slamming loudly against the floor. She lowered it gently onto the granite flagstones and stepped back. The table remained motionless, trying to fly through the solid floor. Sari smirked. City-dwellers thought they were so clever.

But they never thought far enough. She picked up the box again and lifted it over the velvet rope.

Suddenly, she felt something snake around her ankle. She looked down and saw it was the velvet rope, coiling around her legs.

"Monkey droppings!"

Sari quickly put the box down and pushed it, sending it sliding across the floor, out of the rope's reach. Sheer, Cloud and Jewel dived forwards, sinking their teeth into the rope. Sari reached for the weapons in her belt, but the rope looped around her wrists and pulled her hands together, holding them away from her waist just as she had expected. Sari reached into her sleeve and drew her obsidian knife from her wrist sheath. The razor-sharp, black glass blade sliced through the rope like soft fruit. Sari freed herself with two further strokes and jumped out of its grip. The tigers padded back as well. The severed ends of the rope stretched towards them, but couldn't reach far enough. Sari snorted, sheathed her knife, and picked up the box once again, heading for the room's other door.

It was a basic rule of theft – one of thousands Sari had learnt during hundreds of burglaries – that you never left a robbery the same way you had come in. Sari took different corridors and another staircase back down to the second floor. Cloud led the way, his nose and ears open for danger. Sheer and Jewel walked on either side of Sari, ready to protect her as she walked as quickly as she could with her arms wrapped around the box. It was not heavy – in fact, it was very big for whatever was inside it, sliding around loose in the bottom – but it was large enough to be awkward to carry, especially with the sharp stone edges. But another rule of theft was that you did not stop to rest while escaping with the loot. They reached the first floor and were heading in the direction of the next staircase.

"Well, I don't see why we have to wear these amulets!"

Sari froze and so did the tigers. They were three-quarters of the way along the corridor. There were windows that looked out over the garden on one side and on the other a wall with nothing but a side table, three chairs and a small, silver framed mirror. There was nowhere to hide. A second voice and two pairs of brisk footsteps echoed closer.

"Stop playing with it! You need it. Whoever

drugged that poor guardsman and frightened the dogs might still be in here somewhere, so we've got to check every room."

Sari cursed under her breath. Museum magicians! The amulets had to be shrouding charms, which would hide their auras from criminal magicians and would also stop the tigers from smelling them. Sari stood petrified as the two men rounded the corner.

"Fine! But I'm still not…"

The two magicians, a tall one and a short one, strode into view, their long purple robes trailing along the floor behind them. They both jumped in astonishment when they saw Sari.

"Hello," said Sari, in a trembling tone.

"What in the name of…?" said the short magician. The tall one looked shocked, but he recovered himself quickly.

"Uh… Don't move a muscle!" he ordered, holding out his hands. "Give me that exhibit!"

"You're the boss," said Sari, and threw the box towards him.

"Aaah!" The tall magician caught it awkwardly, stumbled backwards over his own robe and fell over.

"By the Stork!" yelled the short one. He thrust

his right arm towards Sari. A glowing blue sphere of magic shot out of his palm and flew towards her. The tigers scattered in three directions. Sari did a back flip over the top of the spell and landed on her feet, flicking a red Sleeping Snake dart at the magician.

"Aargh!" The magician ducked under the dart at the last second and threw a red spell back at her.

"Get her, Archibald!" yelled the tall magician, struggling to sit up with the box on his chest.

Sari did a sideways cartwheel out of the way of the spell onto one of the chairs. She stepped from it onto the table and snatched the silver mirror from the wall. As the magician launched a third spell at her, Sari spun around, thrusting the mirror into its path. The ball of magic bounced off the silvery glass straight back the way it had come. It hit the short magician in the forehead and he dropped unconscious to the floor.

"Oh, merciful Stork!" The tall magician tried again to sit up, pushing the box off his chest to free his arms so he could use his own magic.

"GGGGGGGGGGRRRRRRRRRRRR!!!"
"AAAAHH!!!"

Jewel, Cloud and Sheer all pounced on the magician at once, pinning his arms to the floor before he could throw a spell at Sari. Sari leapt in between them and plunged another dart into the side of the magician's neck. His eyes rolled back and closed.

Sari shook her head and pocketed the dart. Security had improved, but not enough. It would never be enough to stop her. She bent to pick up the box.

"All right. I admit it. That was impressive."

Sari stood bolt upright, leaving the box on the floor. She threw the mirror like a discus, aiming at the tall blue curtains hanging over the corridor windows.

"OUCH!" yelled the voice, as the mirror struck its intended target.

"Mr Leader?!" said Sari.

The curtain was pulled back from the inside, revealing the Leader and his three cohorts, all in their brown uniforms and masks.

"Oww! Yes, it's us," said the Leader, rubbing a growing lump on his forehead. "Good evening, my dear."

"What are you doing here?" said Sari.

"Observing your progress," said the Leader. "As I said, we had no guarantee you could actually pull this off, so I thought we'd better tag along in case anything went wrong. That way, we could grab the—"

"Sir," said Mira.

"Be here to assist you, I mean," said the Leader, "should you have needed it."

"Really?" said Sari, placing her hand on her dagger. Cloud, Sheer and Jewel all growled.

"But it seems we weren't needed," said the Leader, holding out his hands. "You've lived up to your reputation after all, my dear. Now, please. Pass me the casket."

"Where's my money?" said Sari, stepping in front of the box.

"Uaaargh!"

The sudden groan of effort had come from the short magician.

"Look out!" Sari shouted. She did a handspring out of the way as he launched a red combat spell in their direction.

"Sir! Get down!" yelled Hara.

"Don't worry! I've got it!" said the Leader, stepping forwards and drawing his dagger, holding up the polished blade to use as a mirror.

"No! Don't!" shouted Sari.

It was too late. The Leader was already holding the dagger out in the spell's path and the swirling ball of magic hit it. But instead of bouncing backwards, the curved blade sent it shooting off at an angle.

"Waaah!" Etan just ducked in time as the spell flew over his head and sailed down the corridor, through the door of an exhibit room labelled THE HISTORY OF FIREWORKS.

"Oh, Vulture!" said the Leader.

BOOM! BOOM! BOOM! BOOM! BOOM!

The windows shattered and the floor shook. Orange, green, pink and purple lights burst into the corridor. Sari dived to the floor between Sheertooth and Cloudclaw as fireworks streaked, hissing and shrieking up and down the corridor.

"AAARGH! VULTURE'S CURSES!" screamed the Leader as a green and red Catherine wheel hit him in the face.

The tigers snarled and yelped as hot sparks fell like rain and burnt their fur. Shielding her eyes with her hand, Sari squinted through the heat and smoke and spotted the box, still sitting beside the unconscious tall magician. She crawled towards it. This job had gone to pieces faster than a coconut falling from a tree onto a large flat rock, and all thanks to her own client! But she had never failed to complete a job, and she was not about to start now. Sari gripped the box and stood up. Fireworks were still streaming out of the exhibit room, blocking the way to the stairs. There was only one thing for it.

"Come on, guys!" Sari shouted to the tigers.

Sheer, Cloud and Jewel raced to her sides. Together, they ran forwards and jumped out through one of the broken windows.

By an extraordinary piece of luck, they landed on top of a tall and leafy cherry tree. Sari crashed down through the branches, tearing off leaves and fruit, still clutching the box. She dropped out of the bottom and landed lightly on her feet. Sheer, Cloud and Jewel came tumbling out of the tree and landed behind her. Sari quickly checked they were all right and then looked upwards. Pillars of sparks, smoke and fire were pouring out of the broken windows on the first floor. She could hear alarm bells ringing and guards shouting. It was definitely time to go.

Sari and the tigers ran across the lawn, dodging around the flaming patches of grass set alight by falling fireworks. Sari cursed under her breath. Never before had she worked for anyone so breathtakingly stupid as—

"MISS STORMSTRONG!"

Sari stopped. The Leader, Hara and Mira came running across the grass towards her, their brown clothes covered in soot. Etan was hopping behind them, trying to pat out the flames on his right trouser leg. The Leader reached her first. A large piece of his brown cloth headscarf had been torn off by the Catherine wheel, revealing extremely pale skin, apart from the sun-burnt oval around his eyes and nose which wasn't usually covered by his mask.

"Thank the Vulture!" said the Leader. "You managed to save the casket! Now please, give it to me. We need to be gone before the guards or the Royal Protectors arrive."

"Sure," said Sari, keeping a tight hold of the box. "That'll be twelve thousand gold pieces."

"What?" The Leader blinked. "Oh, for Vulture's sake, young lady! I didn't bother to bring it! Hand it over. I'll pay you tomorrow."

"Not a chance," said Sari. She stepped back keeping the box out of reach. Sheertooth, Cloudclaw and Jeweltail moved in front of her and growled.

"What?!" said the Leader.

"I don't work for free, Mr Leader," said Sari. "Until you pay up, the box stays with us."

"Not on your life!" said the Leader, as he took a step forward. Sari shifted the box under her arm, freeing one hand so she could flick her last Sleeping Snake dart into his shoulder.

"OW! WHAaaaaaahh," said the Leader, as the venom took effect.

"Damn you, girl!" said Mira. She and Hara leapt forward and caught the Leader under his armpits before he hit the ground. Mira reached for her sword. Sheer, Jewel and Cloud snarled, baring their teeth.

"No! No! Don't!" Etan jumped between Mira and the tigers, waving his arms. "Stop! Sir was right. We can't fight now! The Royal Protectors will be here any minute. We have to go. Please, Miss Stormstrong. We *will* pay you."

"Good," said Sari. "When you do, you can have the box. See you tomorrow."

Nothing ever changed. City-dwellers were still the worst people in the world. Sari turned around, with Sheertooth, Cloudclaw and Jeweltail beside her, and ran away into the night.

Four

The next morning, the sky over Shirazar was bright and clear. Dew clung to the grass and covered the leaves of the trees in the western park as the Rainbow Carpet cruised overhead. Apart from the slight smell of gunpowder that was drifting from the museum, the air was fresh and cool.

"What kind of moron decides to start a fireworks display by himself in the middle of the night?" said Zal, who was in the pilot's place with Rip beside him.

"The hotel clerk said the night watchman tripped and dropped his lantern in the fireworks exhibit or something," said Zara. She was behind him, reading her tourist scroll again. "Let's go south. I want to see the Fountain of Feathers at the Great Stork Temple first."

"Oh, that's boring," said Zal. "Can't we go to the Arch of Champions? We're not that far from where the race will start."

"Zal, we agreed," said Zara. "Sightseeing in the morning, training in the afternoon. Let's go. Unless you want to practise by yourself."

"OK. Fine."

Zal pushed down with one hand on the soft pile of the carpet, turning it south. It was a beautiful day. The clear sky and crisp air made it almost a perfect morning for flying. Zal pushed down with his other hand and felt the carpet push back against him as it rose up. The Rainbow Carpet was as flat and even as a table top and it felt as solid as sitting on a stone floor. The wind whistled past his ears as the carpet sped up. The seven colours of the carpet glowed bright and vibrant in the morning light and the carpet's magic sparkled like stardust among the woven threads.

"Where do you want to go after that?"

"I haven't decided yet. But probably—"

Zara broke off, as a small yellow flower petal

70

floated past the carpet. Zal blinked. He and Zara turned their heads to follow it. It wasn't unusual to see leaves or flowers carried by the wind while flying, but this petal was different. It was glowing with yellow magic.

"Did you see…?"

Another petal flew past the carpet, and then another. Suddenly, dozens of them were turning and spinning in the air all around them, like falling cherry blossoms, only they were falling up instead of down. Most were yellow, but lots of violet ones were among them. Both sorts were glowing with magic.

"Wow!" said Zara. The sight was strange, but very beautiful.

"What are they?" said Zal.

"I don't know." Zara reached out and tried to catch one, but the petal slipped easily between her fingers like water. However its aura touched hers, and she could tell it was filled with yellow magic. All yellow magic was part of the yellow shade and Zara recognized it easily. It was inside the yellow stripe on the carpet, inside her in her own magic and in the sunlight all around them. But the petal also felt empty, like a seashell, as if there was a space inside it waiting to be filled. "I don't think it's dangerous."

Dozens of flower petals were flowing past the carpet now in moving curtains. Rip sniffed at any that came close to the carpet's edge. Zara peered over the edge, but they were so high above the streets that it was impossible to see where they were coming from.

"What are they?" said Zal, again. "What's going… OH, HOLY STORK ON A SUNBEAM! ZARA!"

"What?" Zara jumped at Zal's sudden outburst.

"LOOK!" Zal pointed down at the carpet.

Close to the edges, the petals were brushing the carpet. Now that Zara looked at them properly she saw they were coming away from it bigger and glowing brighter than before. But the seven colours in the carpet were fading and becoming dull and flat. The tiny glittering jewels of magic were disappearing from amongst the weaving like stars going out.

"THEY'RE STEALING THE CARPET'S MAGIC!" shouted Zal.

"Oh, Holy Stork!" said Zara, as she saw he was right. At that same moment, they both froze as the normally solid Rainbow Carpet began to soften underneath them.

72

"GET US OUT OF HERE!!!" she yelled.

Zal spun around and punched both his palms into the carpet. The Rainbow Carpet lurched forwards through the cloud of flower petals, its corners flapping in the air. Rip yelped and jumped into Zal's lap as he felt his paws sinking into the carpet. Zal pushed harder as the Rainbow Carpet rippled, rising and falling like the surface of the sea. It felt like trying to fly through treacle.

"Zara?"

"Hold on!"

Zara scooted around onto her knees and pressed her hands against the carpet. Her magic blazed inside her like rainbow fire. It flowed down her arms, through her palms and out of her fingers into the weaving. The carpet glowed and then grew steadier as fresh magic flowed through the threads, lighting up the colours once more.

"Oh, Stork!" said Zal, as the air grew thick with more and more flower petals, which flowed past the carpet even faster than before. The colours faded as the magic started to drain from the carpet again.

"Go faster!" said Zara, straining. Sweat flowed down her forehead as she poured magic into the carpet as fast as the petals could suck it out.

"I'm trying!" shouted Zal, as a tornado of flower petals spun up around them. They were trapped in a spinning column of yellow and violet, so thick that for a second, they could not see the sky. Zal sucked in his breath and pushed forward with all his might. The carpet burst through the tornado, sending petals flying. Zal breathed out with relief, and then felt the carpet flap loosely beneath him. He looked down to see that its colours were almost grey.

"WRAFF, WRAFF!"

"OH, STORK!"

Gravity kicked in and the carpet began to fall. Only Zara's magic prevented them from plummeting directly downwards. The carpet fell front end first in a steep, sloping death-dive, hurtling down towards the city.

"OH, CAMELPAAAAAAAAAAT!"

Zal threw himself flat on the carpet, holding onto Rip with one arm and the front edge of the carpet with the other. He held on, cursing the Spring Sparrow, Forest Flamingo, the Precipice Pelican and every other minor bird god he could think of. Zara lay beside him, pouring in all the magic she could summon through her white knuckles. The red stone wall of the park rushed up to meet up them and they shot over it with centimetres to spare, into one of Shirazar's large marketplaces.

Camels honked, horses neighed and a cage of monkeys hooted as the Rainbow Carpet burst into their midst. A potter broke a vase, a stonemason dropped a tombstone on his toes and a hairdresser nearly cut his customer as the carpet's slipstream washed over them, flaring the coloured awnings of their stalls. Zal and Zara squeezed their eyes shut and held on as they tore through the roof of a slipper-maker's stall, smashed through a rack of fruit and vegetables, crashed through a cage of squawking chickens and finally plunged with a splash into an enormous tank of water outside a fishmonger's stall.

Water rushed up Zal's nose and bubbles swirled before his eyes. He tasted salt as he almost sighed underwater with immense relief. The tank had saved them from being splattered across the pavement. Zal turned to follow Zara and Rip, who were swimming up to the surface, and found himself staring into the round, black, frightened eyes of a dozen live octopuses, huddled together in one corner of the tank, their tentacles trembling with fear.

"NO!" shouted Zal. It came out as a stream of bubbles.

The octopuses all released their ink at once. The water in the tank turned black.

"Come on, come on! Work, work, work!"

"Try over there, Zal. More water."

They were back in the hotel suite and the Rainbow Carpet was spread over the table. Zara stood beside Arna with Rip in her arms. They watched as Zal and Augur worked frantically over the Rainbow Carpet with sponges and buckets of rose water. Large pools of inky water lay on the floor around them, ruining the hotel's expensive rugs. Zara shifted her weight between her feet. Rip moaned in her arms and Arna chewed his beard. Zal and Augur were oblivious to the tension, as they were wrapped up in their carpet-weavers' concentration, working to save the Rainbow Carpet.

"Oh, it's no good!" Augur stepped back and lowered his sponge. "That's all we can get off."

"No, no! Keep going!" said Zal, scrubbing harder. "We can save it! We've got to!"

"Zal, stop. You're making it worse," said Augur. "The ink's already soaked deep into the threads. We weren't fast enough."

The furious fishmonger had pulled Zal, Zara and Rip out of the tank, yelling at them for scaring his octopuses. He had been even angrier when they dived straight back in and swam down to the bottom to rescue the Rainbow Carpet. As soon as they had hauled it to the surface, soaking wet, heavy with salt water and entirely covered in sticky black ink, they saw there was no chance of getting it to fly. Zal and Zara had rolled it up, carried it on their shoulders and run non-stop all the way back to the hotel with Rip leading the way. Augur and Arna had almost choked on their breakfast when their children had burst in, covered in ink themselves, yelling for them to get the emergency carpet-cleaning supplies out.

"Oh, camelpat!" Zal ran his hand through his ink-stained hair. "Now we're finished!"

Zara stepped forward and forced herself to look at the Rainbow Carpet. She gasped. Rip whined and buried his face in Zara's elbow. The sides of the Rainbow Carpet were as black as midnight.

The middle, where Zal and Augur had tried their hardest, was a mottled patchwork of different shades of grey, some dark and some light. Not one speck of the seven colours of magic could be seen anywhere.

"Can you re-enchant it, Zara?" said Augur.

"Not in this state, I can't," said Zara. "Black's not one of the seven colours. It needs to be the right colours before I can put magic into it."

She touched the carpet. Just this morning, it had been brimming with magic and she had felt a living, tingling connection between the magic inside it and the magic inside her. But now with the ink in the way, and with most of the magic stolen by the flower petals, it felt cold and empty, like touching an old grey cloth.

"We're finished!" said Zal again, dropping his sponge to the floor.

"Now, now. Let's not panic," said Arna. "This isn't a disaster… Well, OK, yes, it is. But it's not the end of the world! We've got two dozen spare rainbow carpets. You can just race on one of those."

"That's not the same, Dad," said Zara. "Those are just rainbow carpets. This is *the* Rainbow Carpet. It's special. It's the first one we wove, the one we went through the Fire City to get. It's *our* carpet."

Rip yapped in agreement.

"And we might not be allowed to," said Zal. "I read through the rule book before we came. Competitors are meant to race on the exact same means of flight used to win their kingdom's championship race. It's an anti-cheating measure. They won't let us fly on another one."

"Surely they'd make an exception for this?" said Augur.

"I'm not so sure, my friend," said Arna. "You know what sticklers the Shirazans are for detail. Remember how much fine print there was on the breakfast menu?"

"We've got to find a way to fix it," said Zal, touching the carpet himself. "Is there anything you can do with magic?"

"Ummm … maybe," said Zara. "There might be a way, but I don't know what."

"Why not?"

"No one's ever taught me a getting-ink-out-of-a-magic-carpet spell," said Zara. "I'm not even sure if there is such a thing."

"Well, we've got to do something!" said Zal. "We

can't just stand here and wait for the ink to dry."

"No, you should both wash before you do anything else," said Arna, looking at the trail of black footprints they had left across the floor. "Oh, why couldn't this have happened in Azamed? There we'd have high magicians who understand carpet magic to consult about this."

"Wait, Dad. That's it!" said Zara. "High magicians!"

"Where?" said Arna, looking over his shoulder.

"No, they're who we need," said Zara. "High magicians know all the seven colours and all kinds of advanced spell casting. Shirazan magicians don't know much about carpet magic, but if there is a way to do it, they should be able to tell us!"

"Well, that's great," said Zal, "but we don't know any magicians here."

"Don't worry," said Zara, "I know where to find them."

"By the Celestial Stork's beak!" Professor Maltho stared at the Rainbow Carpet with open-mouthed horror. "What on earth did you do to it?"

The Professor was a tall, handsome man in his

forties. He had wavy black hair that came down to his jaw and wore a monocle in his right eye. His long purple robes were those of a senior teacher at the Magicians' Academy, the huge white castle in the middle of the city. It seemed to be a lot bigger on the inside than it was on the outside and because of the many powerful magicians who worked there, it probably was. The Academy was one of the greatest schools of magic in the Seventeen Kingdoms and offered classes in every branch of magic from astro-numerology to frogspawn applications.

"We didn't do it deliberately," said Zal.

"I should hope not!" said the Professor. "Good grief! What a calamity!"

"Can magic fix it, Professor?" said Zara. "There must be some way."

They were standing in the Professor's study, which was a large room, high up on the fifth floor of a tall turret. The mid-morning sun poured in through its narrow windows and reflected off the complicated alchemy sets that covered tables and workbenches. Potions in all seven colours of magic flowed along thin glass tubes and bubbled, boiled or froze inside flasks. A large yellow sofa, made of Windtree wood from Pursolon, floated gently in the corner of the room. Strange rocks and crystals lined the shelves next to stacks of scrolls, jars of coloured powders and a dragon's skull. A map of star constellations and a diagram of a rainbow hung on the walls beside a small oil painting of the Professor with his wife and children.

"Oh, certainly," said the Professor. "There's no doubt about that."

He picked up a magnifying glass and studied the carpet's blackened weaving more closely.

"In its simplest form, magic is nothing more than the power of our brains over the seven shades that make up the natural world. Therefore, anything we can imagine is possible through magic."

"Thank Stork for that!" said Zal. "So you can fix it? We're saved!"

"Unfortunately, no," said the Professor. "It's certainly possible to remove the ink with magic, but I'm afraid I can't do it for you. A magic carpet like this is as much a work of art as it is a means of flight. Only the magician who enchanted it in the first place can carry out such major repair work."

"Me?" said Zara. "But I don't know how! I'm not a high magician."

"We came here because we thought you'd know," said Zal.

"I'm sorry you've had a wasted trip," said the Professor. "But that's the way it is. This isn't like washing a food stain out of a tunic or scraping mud off your shoes. It's more like trying to repair a painting that's been smudged or a statue that's had its nose broken off. Only the artist who painted or sculpted it can restore it to exactly the way it was. If I, or any other magician, were to try, Stork knows what we might do to it by accident."

"Oh no!" said Zal, grabbing the carpet. "It's been through enough! Zara, you have to do it."

"But I don't know how," said Zara. "I'm a seventh-year student. I don't know rainbow dynamics or external shade casting yet. I don't know where to begin."

"You're just going to have to find a place to begin," said the Professor. "Since there's no such thing as a spell for removing octopus ink from a seven-colour magic carpet, you're going to have to invent one. And it has to be one that will work specifically for *this* carpet."

"But how?" said Zara. "I don't know any spells like that."

She looked at the blackened carpet again. Normally, it was easy to use her magic in any of the seven shades. She just needed to look at something that was one of the seven colours, then look inside and find that colour within herself. Then she could send it out, down her arms and through her hands into whatever it was, filling it with magic. But her magic washed over the black and grey Rainbow Carpet like water flowing over a stone. The ink felt like a solid wall that she couldn't hope to break through.

"Look, you said 'with magic'," said Zal. "What about 'without magic'? Is there any other way we could do it?"

"I should be asking you that. You're the carpet-weaver," said Professor Maltho. He stroked his chin and looked at the black and grey Rainbow Carpet again. "But … I suppose you might – and I do mean *might* – try using Rivertree balm. That may be able to get the ink off."

"Rivertree balm?" said Zara.

"It's a special potion that alchemists use for cleaning their lab robes after messy experiments," said the Professor. "It's made of five different ingredients that are all magical, but when they are mixed together they cancel each other out. It's ideal for washing out magic potions before they can stain."

"That sounds perfect," said Zal.

"Wait a minute," said Zara. "What's the risk?"

"It might work too well," said the Professor. "It could wash off the ink, but also wash the dye out of the threads. You could be left with a white carpet, instead of black and grey one, that still won't fly."

"Oh," said Zara.

"But if you can't do a spell, it's better than anything else we've got," said Zal. "And we've got four days until the race."

"I'll write down the recipe for you," said the Professor. "Though, now you mention it, the race might be the bigger problem."

"How?" said Zal.

"Those mysterious flower petals you saw," said the Professor. "We had better find out what they were before the race in case they strike again."

The Professor went over to the tall set of shelves that held his library. They were filled with dozens of scrolls on magic, and also writing tablets made of stone, wax and clay. There were rocks carved all over with strange symbols, and spells written in charcoal on sheets of tree bark or in blood on animal skins by the earliest magicians. One shelf even contained several of the peculiar piles of paper, glued together along one side between thick sheets of card and made in the far western kingdoms, called books. The Professor lifted down one of these volumes with a brown leather cover and carried it over to a table. Zal and Zara stood beside him as he turned over the cover, revealing the title, *Methods for the Stealing of Magic.*

"If any magician has ever encountered them before, they should be recorded in here," said the Professor, turning the pages. The book was written in thick paragraphs of swirling handwriting, divided up by beautifully drawn and coloured pictures.

"Just how many methods are there to steal magic?" said Zara. The pictures showed magicians losing their powers to demons, having their shades sucked out into cursed jars or running in terror from packs of magic-inhaling aardvarks.

"Far too many," said the Professor. "And each one can be achieved in a number of different ways. We need to narrow it down to—"

"Hey, wait!" said Zal. "That's it!"

They looked down at the page. The picture showed a beautiful girl in a long blue dress, kneeling with her head bowed and her eyes closed, as she held up a vase of yellow and violet flowers. The flowers were shedding their petals, which were not falling, but flying up into a swirling storm above the girl's curling red hair.

"What?!" said Professor Maltho, looking shocked.

"That's them. Those are the flower petals," said Zal.

"Definitely," said Zara. "Well done, Zal... Professor?"

"Those?!" said the Professor, with wide eyes. "Are you absolutely sure? Someone used the Crystal Flowers of Kandara on you this morning?"

"What are they?" said Zara.

"By the Stork's feathers! Oh, they're an ancient magical weapon," said the Professor. "They were created by the magician-princess Kandara five thousand years ago. She used them to defend her kingdom from a horde of giant man-eating bats. But someone used them on you? By the River Robin!"

"Why? Are they meant to be lost in the winds of time beyond the mists of history or something?" said Zal, remembering how the secret to weaving rainbow carpets had been lost for thousands of years in Azamed before he and Zara had come along.

"No, they're meant to be right here," said the Professor. "They're kept in the Academy's own museum. But they were stolen from it a month ago!"

"Stolen?" said Zara.

"Yes, someone broke into the museum in the middle of the night and made off with the whole vase," said the Professor. "They picked all the locks, including the picking-proof ones, and walked through every security spell like they weren't there. The only clues those fools in the Royal Protectors managed to find were some strands of black and orange fur inside the broken display case. It was the most audacious episode in the crime wave yet."

"The crime wave?" said Zal.

"Oh, of course. I forgot you wouldn't know about it. You were still in Azamed when it started," said the Professor.

He went over to his parchment-strewn desk and dug out a copy of a news scroll. Zal read the title —

The Shirazar Star – and recognized it as the most popular one in the kingdom.

"It's been going on for three months," said the Professor, unrolling it. "A string of seemingly impossible burglaries all over Shirazar. The Royal Protectors don't want to admit they're baffled."

The middle section of the scroll contained a two-foot long report on the crime wave. Beside it, there was a list in date order of every item that had been stolen so far with small pictures of each one drawn beside it.

"The Vessel of Tears, the Mirror Curtain, the Crystal Flowers of Kandara, the Moon Bow, the Demon Chessmen, the Fire Scimitar and the Boomerang of Astigor," read Zal, reading the list backwards from the most recent theft. "Holy Stork! What are all these things?"

"Whatever they are, they don't sound safe," said Zara.

"Most of them aren't," said the Professor. "What someone could want them all for is anyone's guess. The only things they have in common are that they're all old, valuable, magical and one-of-a-kind. But now that I think about it…"

"What is it, sir?" said Zal.

"Gentle Stork," said the Professor, stroking his chin. "It's not just the Crystal Flowers of Kandara that could have been used to make you crash. Every one of those items could have been used to bring down almost any means of flight!"

"Every single one of them?" said Zara.

"By the Precipice Pelican!" said the Professor. He looked at Zal and Zara, clearly unnerved. "Could someone be planning to sabotage the Champions' Race?"

Five

By now, it was lunchtime and the streets of Shirazar were busy. People were sitting at tables outside cafés and restaurants, and stalls were selling hot and spicy snacks. Camels, horses, mules and even a pair of elephants were eating from nosebags or drinking from the fountains as Zal and Zara landed on the pavement on one of the spare rainbow carpets.

"What makes you so sure they'll have what we need?" said Zara, as they got off.

"Because they always do," said Zal, as they lifted the ink-ruined rainbow carpet and rolled up the spare one. "There is nothing better for cleaning sword blades. They always have a few big urns in the

91

cellars. Now stand back. I need to do the entrance test."

Professor Maltho had provided them with three of the five ingredients needed to make Rivertree balm. Under her free arm, Zara was carrying a well-wrapped parcel containing dragon-tooth powder, flower-tree resin and lightning ashes. But – with the advanced alchemy students' practical exam happening this week – the Academy had run out of quartz oil from the Crystal Deeps in the eastern desert.

They were standing in front of a narrow building, set well back from the street between two others. Ten stone steps led from the pavement up to the door, which was round and carved in the shape of a lion's mouth. Two crossed scimitars were engraved into the wall above it. Set in the walls on either side of the door were two small fountains, also carved into the shape of lions' mouths, facing each other across the top step. Water gushed from these into two small square pools. A large bronze doorknocker in the shape of a sword pommel was mounted in the middle of the heavy wooden door. They put the carpets down on the step and Zal knocked on the door five times.

"Who goes there?" boomed a deep and dramatic voice from inside.

"Zal Thesa of Azamed!" Zal called. "A foreign student returns to seek his teacher's aid!"

Rip barked beside him. Zara raised her eyebrows.

"Then pass the Trial of Skill and enter, Zal Thesa," said the voice. "Are you ready? Here it comes!"

A small hatch hidden behind the lion's top teeth dropped open and a large pomegranate fell out. Fast as lightning, Zal whipped his sword from its scabbard in a perfect horizontal-draw-cut, slicing the pomegranate in half. The two pieces flew in opposite directions and into the mouths of the two lion fountains, just as their stone jaws snapped shut. The water gurgled as it drained out of the two pools below them. A mechanism clicked and the door swung open.

"Ha, ha! Perfect!" said the deep voice. "Enter and learn all the secrets of the blade! Welcome to the School of Swords! Welcome back, Zal. It's great to see you."

"Thanks, Marto. You too," said Zal, pushing the door open to reveal a young man sitting at a desk next to a huge bronze speaking tube. "Is Mistress Shen in?"

"Teaching the advanced class right now," said the young man, writing Zal's name down in a visitor's book. "Go straight through."

Zara looked around with interest as they walked through the School of Swords, carrying the two carpets. Rip led the way along narrow corridors with bare floorboards. The rooms off the corridor had walls made out of paper screens and sliding doors, which were from Yamaroto. Through the paper, she could vaguely see classes of students sitting in disciplined rows and listening to their teachers in complete silence. They passed a small library that was full of fencing manuals and biographies of famous swordsmen. There was even a small blacksmith's shop where the students could get their swords sharpened or learn to make their own.

"So this is where you used to train?" said Zara.

"Yes. It's the greatest fencing school in the world," said Zal. "Every technique in every sword style that's ever existed is taught here. I used to want to move permanently to Shirazar just so I could live here."

At the end of the corridor a green silk curtain, embroidered with another lion hung over the doorway and they could hear swords clashing on the other side. Rip scampered under it as Zal brushed it aside, and they stepped through onto the wooden balcony that ran around the walls of the main training hall.

Two dozen students of about Zal's age, both boys and girls, were hard at work. Some stood before long mirrors, slowly practising basic sword manoeuvres over and over. Others were practising strikes and cuts on wooden posts or complicated training dummies that would spin around when they were hit. Several were rolling about in pairs in pits filled with sawdust, practising wrestling techniques. Two pairs stood on raised fencing platforms fighting practice bouts. Zara felt a ripple of magic as they walked onto the balcony. Around the edges of the hall were small training rooms that the school's magician students had enchanted with different kinds of weather so they could practise fighting in all conditions. Thunder rolled and lightning crackled out of one, a snow-storm swirled inside another and torrential rain hammered down inside a third. In the centre of the room, a tall woman dressed in red was giving instructions.

"Relax your wrist, Jensa. It is a sword, not an axe.

Move it like you'd move a paintbrush, not a meat cleaver."

"Mistress Shen!" cried Zal. He dropped his end of the carpets and he and Rip hurried down the stairs to the training floor.

"Well, well," said the woman, without turning around. "The Champion of Azamed returns to us at last. What took you so long, Thesa?"

"I'm sorry, my teacher. I would have come sooner, but… Oww!" said Zal, breaking off as Mistress Shen suddenly spun around and poked him in the nose with a wooden stick.

"By the Sparrow Gods!" said Mistress Shen, rolling her ocean-green eyes. "How can a student who can complete the Seven Colours Test and the Five Perfects Cuts at such a young age still be so slow? You haven't improved at all since I last saw you, Thesa."

Mistress Shen was tall and elegant, with porcelain-pale skin and shining black hair that hung down to her waist and was held in place by a large golden clip in the shape of a butterfly. She wore two scimitars through the belt of her scarlet robe, their scabbards decorated with dragons.

"I'm sorry, my teacher. I have been trying," said

Zal, bowing and rubbing his nose. "It's just hard when I'm so far away from the school."

"No, it isn't, because I'm not talking about physical speed," said Mistress Shen. "You still haven't learnt to sense intentions. Your mind is as much a weapon as your sword. Your brain and your blade need to work as one. Your senses need to be as sharp as your sword's edge so you can read body language, emotions and expressions and tell what your opponent is about to do. But you're still not thinking any further ahead than your sword's tip."

"I've been telling him that for years," said Zara, as she carried both carpets under her arms down the stairs.

"Then you're wise beyond your age," said Mistress Shen. "And I'm delighted to meet you at last, Zara. I've been listening to Thesa moan about you for years."

"I'm sorry, my teacher. I'll try to do better," said Zal, bowing.

"Stop bowing, you look like a pigeon," said Mistress Shen. "Just remember, Thesa, that being able to sense intentions is the only way to protect yourself against surprise attacks. It's not that hard. Nocturne grasped it the first time I explained it to him."

"Is Miles here?" said Zal, looking around at the practising students.

"No, I was about to ask if you knew where he was," said Mistress Shen. "It's most unlike him to miss a class."

"Zal! Zara!"

"Ah. Speak of the Sparrow Gods."

Zal and Zara looked around as Miles Nocturne ran panting down the stairs. He was red-faced from running and was carrying a sack over his shoulder and Fluffy under his arm.

"Miles!" said Zal.

"Zal!"

CLAAANG!

"Ha! Still slow!" said Miles.

"Camelpat!"

"Zal!" said Zara.

"Sorry. Force of habit," said Zal, sheathing his sword.

"MEOW!" said Fluffy, as she pounced on Rip.

"WRAFF, WRAFF!" said Rip, as the two pets rolled away towards the sawdust pits.

"It's unlike you to be late, Nocturne," said Mistress

Shen. "And it's very inappropriate behaviour for one of my finest students."

"I'm sorry, my teacher. I couldn't help it," said Miles, bowing. "I've been running all over the city looking for these two."

"Why?" said Zara.

"Because I heard a magic carpet crashed in the southern market," said Miles. "Was it you? Are you OK?"

"Yes, that was us," said Zal.

"We're fine," said Zara. "The only casualty was the carpet."

She knelt down and unrolled the Rainbow Carpet, which they had carried in with them. Rip and Fluffy, covered in sawdust, padded back to watch. Miles gasped as he saw the black and grey mess.

"Oh, Holy Stork!" he said. "I am so sorry."

"It wasn't your fault," said Zal. "It was those stupid octopuses. We should have bought them all so we could eat them."

"I take it the carpet is not supposed to look like that?" said Mistress Shen. "What happened?"

"It's a long story," said Zara. "We think someone's trying to sabotage the Champions' Race."

"What?" said Miles, staring at her. "What makes you think that?"

"Someone used a magical weapon to make us crash," said Zal. "It was one of the items stolen in the crime wave. And everything that's been stolen could be used to bring down different means of flight."

"By the Spring Sparrow!" said Mistress Shen. "That would explain why they stole the Fire Scimitar from us three weeks ago."

"Holy Stork, it would make sense," said Miles. "Do you have any proof? Anything at all?"

"No," said Zara. "Not yet, anyway."

"It doesn't matter. We can't tell anyone until we've fixed the carpet," said Zal. "If we do, they'll just say we're making it up to try to get the race postponed until we can fly again. That's why we came here, Mistress Shen. We need to borrow some quartz oil for the potion that can clean it."

"You shall have it," said Mistress Shen. "Jensa! Go down to the basement and fetch the oil urn."

"But my teacher! I cleaned my sword last night!"

"Don't argue with me! Go and get it!"

"Thank you so much, Mistress Shen," said Zara.

"You can clean it? That's good news," said Miles. "I'd feel awful if you were kept out of the race."

"We still need one more thing," said Zara. She unrolled the recipe scroll Professor Maltho had given her. "I can mix the ashes, the resin and the dragon-tooth powder with the oil. But then we have to dissolve it all in river water that's been collected as it flows over the roots of a tree growing by the river-bank. Where on earth are we going to find that?"

"Oh, no problem," said Miles. "I know the perfect place."

Ten minutes later, they were hurrying along the pavement towards the Shirazar museum.

"There's a pear tree that grows beside a stream in the gardens around the back," said Miles. "We used to play there when we were small. Don't you remember?"

"I just remember losing," said Zal. He and Miles had spent hours chasing each other around the museum gardens with their wooden swords during his first visits to Shirazar and it was the time Miles had started beating him at the diagonal-draw-cut.

"Is it a natural stream?" said Zara. "If it's been dug for decoration, the magic might not be strong enough."

"No, it's a real one," said Miles. "It was here before the museum was built and probably before Shirazar was built. Let's just hope the museum's not closed after the accident last night."

"You know about it too?" said Zal.

"The fireworks woke me up," said Miles. "Apparently, the caretaker's dog knocked over the night-watchman's lantern and it rolled into the fireworks room before they could catch it. But that shouldn't take too long to clean up."

"Good," said Zara. "And thanks for coming with us, by the way."

"Oh, don't mention it," said Miles. "Dad's going to be in the race too, remember. If someone's trying to sabotage it, I want to know about it."

They rounded the corner of the museum wall but stopped when they saw the front gates. They were tall and made of wrought iron, crafted into the shapes of flowers and butterflies and were closed and locked with a large padlock. Two Royal Protectors were standing in front of them in their blue armour, holding tall spears.

"What on earth?" said Zara.

"What's going on?" said Zal.

"I don't know," said Miles. "Unless... Oh, Stork."

"What?" said Zal, looking at him.

"Maybe last night's accident wasn't an accident," said Miles.

They looked through the gates behind the two Royal Protectors, where they could see more blue-armoured officers, carefully searching the grass in front of the museum.

"Well, whatever it was, we still need the water," said Zara.

"It doesn't look like they're going to let us in, though," said Zal.

"Don't worry. Leave this to me," said Miles. "Just follow my lead."

He straightened his tunic and marched smartly down the pavement, straight up to the gates and saluted.

"Good afternoon, sirs!" he said. "Cadet Nocturne, Miles. Number 5479. Royal Protector Cadets reporting for special duty."

"What special duty?" said one of the Royal Protectors. "We weren't told you were coming."

"That's strange, sir. I received the orders by carrier pigeon twenty minutes ago," said Miles. "I've been on escort duty for our special guests, Cadets Thesa and Aura, from the Caliph of Azamed Guard Cadets."

"It's a pleasure to make your acquaintance, sir!" said Zal, standing up straight and saluting. "May I say what a great honour it is to be invited to assist our opposite numbers in Shirazar."

"I didn't know Azamed had a cadet corps," said the second Royal Protector, frowning.

"Newly formed, sir," said Zal. "Captain Burs, the head of the Caliph's Guard, decided to found our branch six months ago on Shirazar's example."

"Never mind that. What orders?" said the first Royal Protector.

"They said you urgently needed a sniffer dog, sir," said Miles. "Rip here is the best in Azamed."

"Wraff, wraff!" said Rip.

"We haven't been told anything about that," said the second Royal Protector.

"Really, sir? That's odd," said Miles. "The message was signed by Captain Curta, Captain Danso and Captain Kalin."

"OK! Right! Good! Come straight in!" The first Royal Protector spun around immediately to unlock the gate, looking nervously around for his senior officers.

"You'll find the captains in the investigation tent," said the second Royal Protector, as he ushered them through. "Report to them immediately, Cadets."

"Yes, sir!" said Zal. "Understood perfectly, sir!"

They quickly hurried up the gravel path through the garden.

"Well done," Miles whispered once they were out of earshot. "Just keep acting like cadets and we'll be fine."

"Sure," said Zal. "So remember to salute next time, Zara!"

"You didn't show me how!" said Zara, as they approached the museum buildings. The windows on the third floor of the east wing had been blown out. The edges of the wall were blackened where fire had raged out of control, before the Shirazan fire brigade had arrived with a flock of specially trained water dragons to put it out. Scorched pieces of wood from broken window frames were scattered across the lawn along with globules of glass that had melted into strange shapes in the intense heat. A dozen or so more Royal Protectors were marking the positions of every single one of them with small blue flags stuck in the grass. Beneath the broken windows, a trio of officers were taking statements from the museum's magicians, two of whom had bandaged foreheads.

"Holy Stork," said Zal.

"They're not treating it like any accident I've seen," said Miles. "No doubt about it. This is something bigger. Maybe even—"

"Wraff, wraff!"

They looked around. Rip was snuffling in the grass at the edge of the path. He stopped and froze for a moment, with his nose pressed to the ground, his big brown eyes growing wider. Then he took off running across the lawn, barking again.

"Rip?" said Zal.

"What is it?" said Miles, as they followed.

"He's found a scent!"

Ducking behind trees and bushes to stay out of sight of the Royal Protectors, they followed Rip through the garden and around the corner to the western side of the museum. He galloped across the grass, following the scent towards a flowerbed that ran in front of a tall apple tree. He stopped at the edge of the flowerbed and jumped up and down, barking at something in the middle.

"How has he found a scent? We don't know what to look for," said Zara.

"It must be something he recognizes. What is it, boy?" said Zal, as they caught up and he could see the object in the flowerbed too. "What is that?"

"Zal, wait!" Miles grabbed Zal's arm as he reached towards it and several of the flowers snapped shut beneath his fingers.

"Holy Stork!" said Zal, snatching his arm back.

"Gothopari Feeding Flowers," said Miles. "They planted them after the museum was burgled two weeks ago."

"Never mind. We need to get that – whatever it is!" said Zal, peering at it.

He drew his sword and used it to reach into the flowerbed. Several of the blossoms snapped shut around it and sliced their petals off on the razor-sharp blade. Zal hooked the tip under the object and then lifted it up into the light where they could see it.

"HOLY STORK!"

Zal and Zara went white and their expressions

went from amazement to disbelief and then to fear.

"WRAAAAFF!" said Rip, looking much the same.

"Meow?" said Fluffy.

"It can't be," said Zara. "It can't be. Not here!"

"What's wrong?" said Miles. "It's just a headscarf, isn't it?"

He was right. It was a long, thin length of cloth, wide enough to be wrapped around the head for protection against the blowing desert sands. One of its edges was rough and moist, where it had been half chewed by the flowers. The other end was black and sooty and smelled of fireworks. But they could still see what colour it had been. It was the same shade of brown used by the Shadow Society.

"Really, Miss Aura! Do you realize how ridiculous this story is?" said Lord Dasat.

Lord Dasat was Azamed's ambassador to Shirazar, a distant cousin of the Caliph. He was a tall, thin man with a hooked nose, a grey beard and an annoyed expression, which had been getting worse since he had arrived ten minutes ago.

"Sir, we've brought you the proof," said Zara, laying the headscarf on the table.

"No, you have not!" said Lord Dasat. "You've brought me a piece of cloth that could have come from anywhere. It's not even evidence. Let alone proof."

"Calm down, Lord Ambassador," said Captain Curta of the Royal Protectors. "True, it is only a piece of cloth, but it was found at the crime scene and I need to take it into account."

They were standing in a tent on the museum lawn. Several folding tables and workbenches had been set up inside it and were now covered with carefully labelled pieces of firework-scorched evidence. A hastily drawn map of the crime scene hung from one wall. Captain Curta, a tall, sandy haired man with a moustache and the scars of several sword fights, was sitting at the head of the table. He had sent for the Ambassador as soon as Miles had introduced Zal and Zara and explained their theory.

"What is this Shadow Society anyway?" said Miles. "I understand it's something bad, but I have no idea what it is."

"Was," said Lord Dasat, before anyone else could answer. "It no longer exists. The Shadow Society was a secretive brotherhood that was recently outlawed in Azamed for its criminal activities. But you don't need to worry about them, Captain. We caught all of them."

"How do you know?" said Zara. "No one ever knew how many there were."

Before their downfall, the Shadow Society only appeared on the streets of Azamed clad in their identical and all-concealing brown uniforms. Zara had only ever learnt to recognize one of them – her nemesis Haragan – and that was only because she had stared into his eyes so often during magic contests.

"We know we have caught them all, Miss Aura, because their nefarious deeds have entirely ceased in Azamed," said Lord Dasat. "The idea that some fugitives are somehow at large here in Shirazar is simply ludicrous."

"You have to admit it's the right colour," said Zal, pushing the headscarf towards him.

"That proves nothing," said Lord Dasat, pushing it back. "The Shadows were not the only people to ever use this shade of brown, Mr Thesa."

"I have to agree with Lord Dasat," said the Captain, picking up the headscarf himself. "It's a strange coincidence finding it here, but that doesn't make it evidence. It's not enough for me to take to the Empress."

"But, sir! My dog recognized their scent!" said Zal.

"I definitely can't take him to the Empress. She's allergic," said Captain Curta. "I'm sorry, Mr Thesa, but there is simply no proof."

"Quite right," said Lord Dasat. "You two helped expose the Shadow Society for the vile wrongdoers they were and you should be very proud of that. But you're letting your imaginations run away with you this time. You're seeing shadows – of Shadows – when there are none."

"Your theory about the crime wave, though, is a different matter," said Captain Curta. "If you're right, we've got a very serious problem."

"I think we're right, sir. It makes perfect sense," said Miles. "We saw how well the Crystal Flowers worked on the Rainbow Carpet, and everything else that's been stolen so far could also be used to take means of flight out of the air."

"What was stolen from the museum this time?" said Zal. "Could that be used as well?"

"I wish I knew," said Captain Curta. "Unfortunately, we have no idea what it is."

"You don't?" said Zara.

"Can't you just count everything in the museum and see what's missing?" said Zal.

"We know what's missing, but we don't know what it is," said the Captain. He pulled a large, heavy scroll labelled "Museum Catalogue" across the table towards him and unrolled it to the middle section. A neatly drawn picture showed a stone box with grooves carved around its sides and writing engraved on its lid. Underneath a record of its measurements, the writing was neatly copied down. Zara frowned at the letters, which were strange, but somehow familiar.

"That's what was stolen, but we have no clue what's inside it," said Captain Curta. "The museum director admitted to me this morning that they were in such a hurry to launch the new exhibition that they put it on display without checking."

"What does it say?" said Zal, looking at the writing.

"I'm afraid we don't know that either," said Captain Curta. "It's a language none of the museum's so-called experts can translate. The box was dug out of the ruins of Jaktivar, but—"

"Jaktivar?" said Zara. "Holy Stork!"

"What's wrong?" said Miles.

"That's it!" said Zara, snapping her fingers. "That's why I recognize the letters!"

"You do?" said Zal.

"You know something that the finest academic minds in Shirazar do not?" said Lord Dasat, raising his eyebrows.

"Fantastic!" said Miles. "What does it say?"

"I don't know," said Zara. "I said I recognized it, not that I can read it. But don't worry, I know someone who can."

Half an hour later, Zal and Zara were standing with Miles and Captain Curta back at Professor Maltho's.

"It's written in ancient High Jaktivarian," said Zara, laying the museum catalogue on the table. "It's a special language that was reserved only for the kings of Jaktivar and their closest advisors, priests and magicians. My teacher translated it for the first time in Azamed last year."

"What a stroke of luck," said Captain Curta. "I can hardly believe it."

"And I can't believe Qwinton's cracked the riddle of ancient High Jaktivarian and then not bothered to tell anyone," said Professor Maltho, pouring water into his speaking bowl. "He knows perfectly well I've been trying to translate it for fifteen years!"

"He probably forgot," said Zal. "He might even have forgotten he translated it."

"Oh, I wouldn't think so," said Zara. "His long-term memory is pretty good. It's just his short-term memory that's bad."

"Let's find out," said Professor Maltho, as he poured a small pot of wind dust into a bowl, which was carved from black obsidian. He stirred it into the water with a wooden spoon and then added a lump of Azamedian volcanic rock, a fresh flower and several grapes collected from the trees at Azamed's Guild of Magicians School. He dipped his hands into the water and closed his eyes. Blue magic glowed around his fingertips. The water in the bowl was reflecting the ceiling of the professor's study. The water rippled as the glow spread and suddenly the reflection changed to a different ceiling in a different city and a different kingdom, hundreds of miles away across the Great Desert.

"Hello, Qwinton? Are you there?" said Professor Maltho.

"What…? AAAAAHHH!" came a voice from the other side. "A GHOST!"

"Stork save us," said the Professor, rolling his eyes.

"Master Qwinton! It's us!" called Zara, leaning over the bowl. "It's Zal and Zara!"

"Zara?"

Qwinton's face appeared, peering down into the bowl. He was a middle-aged man, with wild, curly hair and a thick ruffly beard. As usual, his glasses were askew on his nose, mostly because he was wearing them upside down. Despite being slightly mad due to an accident with a spell years ago, Qwinton was Zara's favourite teacher at the school and her mentor as a magician. She was well used to his absent-mindedness and bizarre trains of thought.

"Yes, Master Qwinton. It's me," said Zara.

"By the Stork's stork! It's you, Zara!" said Qwinton, smiling through the water. "How good to see you! And you look splendid! As if you've just ridden a camel home and eaten it whole. How are you? How's Snowdrift?"

"We're in Shirazar, Master Qwinton, not

Frostbite," said Zara. "But I'm very well, thank you. I need your help, though."

"My help?" said Qwinton. "Well, you can forget it! How dare you make such an impudent request! Anyone would think you were one of my best students."

"Oh, boy," said Zal.

"Is this going to take a while?" said Miles.

"Probably."

"I'm sorry, Master Qwinton, but this is important," said Zara. "It's something only you can do."

"Important? And only I can do it? Oh, well, that changes everything!" said Qwinton. "What do you need? A recipe to make spiced camel steaks out of sand? A way to use parrot feathers to catch a monkey? The secret to finding a long-lost fragment of an ancient Rainbow Carpet? Those are all things only I can do."

"What about translating ancient High Jaktivarian?" said Zal, looking over Zara's shoulder.

"Zal, my boy? What on earth are you doing there?" said Qwinton. "Aren't you meant to be in Shirazar? The Champions' Race has practically started."

"Oh, Holy Stork," said Zal.

"Don't worry, Master Qwinton. He'll make it in time," said Zara. She held the scroll over the bowl. "Can you read this for me?"

"That, my dear? Of course I can! Let's see," came Qwinton's voice from underneath it. "Shirazar Museum Catalogue. Item number 45798. Small Skandian teapot. Colour blue. Decorated with—"

"No. Sorry, Master. Not the whole thing," said Zara. She pointed to the copy of the inscription. "Just this bit."

"What have we here? Ancient High Jaktivarian. What a coincidence!" said Qwinton. "Did you know those addle-brained fools at the Academy in Shirazar have been working on it for fifteen years and they *still* can't figure it out?"

"I'll give you addle-brained, you forgetful bungler!" said Professor Maltho, lunging for the bowl. "Let go of me, Captain!"

"Zara, did you hear something?"

"Never mind, Master. It's not important," said Zara. "What does it say?"

"Ah! Ancient High Jaktivarian. Such a beautiful and complex language. It can keep one awake at night even more than the most diabolical crossword puzzle. Did I ever tell you about—?"

"Master!" said Zara.

"Oh, sorry. What does it say?" said Qwinton. They heard the water gurgle as he adjusted his glasses. "Ah, yes. Very straightforward. It is two lines, Zara, and the first one reads THE CASKET OF THE NIGHT DEMON."

There was a long pause.

"What does the second one say?" said Zara.

"DO NOT OPEN UNDER ANY CIRCUMSTANCES," said Qwinton. "Hmm. Puzzling. I wonder what it means?"

"The Night Demon," said Zal, slowly. "The Night Demon?"

"That doesn't sound good," said Miles, holding Fluffy close to him.

"Do not open under any circumstances," does seem to suggest that," said Professor Maltho.

"No, no! Under ANY circumstances," said Qwinton. "ANY. The grammar's very clear."

"I don't suppose you might have made a mistake in the translation, Sir Magician?" said Captain Curta.

"Certainly not, whoever you are!" said Qwinton. "I decoded this language from its first principles."

"Oh, good," said Captain Curta.

"What do we do now?" said Miles.

"I think that's pretty obvious, Cadet," said the Captain. "We need to find the thieves and the box. Ideally, before they open it."

Six

Deep beneath Shirazar, water dripped from the roof of a dark stone cavern. Stalactites hung from the ceiling with bats roosting among them. A shallow stream flowed through the cavern, branching off to flow around the large dry island in the middle, and then joining together again as the water flowed out. Water dragons with scales that were pure white from never seeing the sun swam in the stream. They plopped under the water out of sight as voices echoed down the tunnel.

"By Salladan's mask!" said the Leader, as he stalked into the cavern from a sloping side tunnel. "Curse that damned mercenary Sari Stormstrong! I can't believe we actually had to pay her!"

"It was her tigers, sir," said Etan, coming in behind him, carrying the box. "When you're eyeball to eyeball with three of them, it's hard to say no."

"What have I told you about making excuses?" said the Leader. "This is a shameful day for us. Oh, well. We can settle things with her soon enough. The important thing is that we've got it."

The Leader took the box from Etan and strode onto the island, oblivious as he splashed through the stream and stepped in a patch of bat droppings, where he placed the box down on a large, flat stone as a big as a table. Around the stone, away from the water, lay the Shadows' sleeping bags and packs of supplies. Etan lit the lanterns that were hanging from the stalactites while the Leader ran his hands over the box and the carved grooves of the inscription.

"At last!" he said.

"What is it, sir?" said Etan.

"The instrument of our revenge," said the Leader. "We have passed the brink of disaster and fallen over the edge. This will enable us to climb back up. How much do you know about the Carpet Wars?"

"Not a lot, sir," said Etan. "History wasn't my best subject in Shadow School."

"Really? What was?"

"Umm…"

"Never mind," said the Leader. He picked up a strong stonemason's chisel and a hammer, lined up the chisel against the crack of the box's lid and started tapping gently.

"The Carpet Wars were fought between Azamed and Jaktivar ten thousand years ago," said the Leader. "Not many people know this, but the craft of weaving flying carpets – not just rainbow carpets, mind you, any flying carpets – was not actually invented in Azamed."

"It wasn't?" said Etan.

"I just told you that," said the Leader. "It was discovered thousands of years earlier, before the founding of Azamed, by the magicians of the Forgotten Empire. They were the creators of magic carpets and they used them to build an empire that sprawled over the entire continent. Before even the Great Desert existed, they ruled these lands with an iron fist. They were the continent's earliest and mightiest civilization."

"What was the Forgotten Empire, sir?" said Etan.

"How should I know? It's why it's called forgotten,"

said the Leader. "From the tales told of their harsh tyranny and endless bloodletting, it was probably forgotten for a good reason. But they ruled most of the known world until the tribe of Asameed – assisted by our great founder, Salladan Shadow – led the other subjugated tribes in rebellion and succeeded in crushing it. Afterwards, they divided up the Empire's lands and founded their own nations in its ashes. The Seventeen Kingdoms we know today are descended from the eighteen tribes that formed the revolt."

"Eighteen?" said Etan. "But—"

"I'm coming to that," said the Leader. He found the chisel wasn't getting through the lid so he moved it to a different position and tried again. "There are Seventeen Kingdoms today because, ten thousand years ago, one was utterly destroyed. That kingdom was Jaktivar, Azamed's rival for control of flying carpets.

"Jaktivar had once been Azamed's closest ally amongst the tribes. Their leaders had stood together like brothers and it was their armies working together that led the final assault on the Forgotten Empire's capital. But that would all change dramatically."

"What happened?" said Etan.

"After the victory, all the tribes returned to their ancestral lands and built their kingdoms. They also started discovering their means of flight. But Azamed and Jaktivar didn't need to do this because they had captured the methods for weaving all types of flying carpets during the campaign. All except rainbow carpets."

"They had rainbow carpets back then?" said Etan.

"Yes, the Forgotten Empire invented them, but the last emperor took the secret to his grave," said the Leader. "But that didn't matter to Azamed and Jaktivar because they were both growing fabulously wealthy by trading on magic carpets. None of the other kingdoms had enough of their own means of flight yet, so merchants from Azamed and Jaktivar made fortunes by flying goods between the other kingdoms. But, as time passed, the weeds of suspicion and rivalry began to grow between them."

"Why?" said Etan.

"Because they were competing with each other in the magic carpet transport market," said the Leader. "They both feared that the other would rediscover the secret to weaving rainbow carpets before they did and put them out of business. Because Azamed is apparently built slightly closer than Jaktivar to where the Forgotten Empire's capital was, the kings of Jaktivar became paranoid that Azamed was going to find the secret first. Over the next two hundred years, the Jaktivarians made several serious attempts to conquer Azamed and capture their magic carpet knowledge."

"So those were the Carpet Wars?" said Etan.

"No, they were the Table Wars. Of course they were the Carpet Wars!" said the Leader. "Ultimately, the Jaktivarians were doomed to fail. The other kingdoms sided with Azamed, and the caliphs had the Shadow Society on their side – even if the ungrateful wretches didn't appreciate it. When the Jaktivarians realized that they couldn't hope to win the war with their army alone, they tried a different course."

"What was that?" said Etan, who was becoming very interested in the story.

"Magic," said the Leader. "Battlefield spell-casting and sorcerous weaponry. The Azamedians responded in kind, of course, and the later wars grew even more deadly – and bizarre – as magicians clashed alongside soldiers. Spells were used as often as cannons, demons and monsters were wielded alongside swords and spears. But it didn't help and for years, they were locked in a stalemate.

"But in the final year of the wars, the Jaktivarians had an idea. The war had begun because of magic carpets. Azamed was using theirs to trade with the other kingdoms for vital supplies and for moving their troops around. If they could only destroy Azamed's carpets faster than they could weave replacements, they could still win the war."

"What did they do?" said Etan.

"The last king of Jaktivar set his magicians to work creating the ultimate, undefeatable, anti-flying carpet weapon. He wanted something that could tear Azamed's carpet fleet to pieces in mid-air. The magicians worked tirelessly for months, trying every possible idea they could conceive, and finally, they succeeded.

"The problem was that the weapon worked too well. The first time they tried it out on some captured Azamedian carpets, it got out of their control and escaped the testing ground into Jaktivar itself. Once it was on the loose in the city, the magicians

126

realized that they hadn't enchanted it to tell the difference between Azamedian carpets and Jaktivarian ones. The weapon did exactly what it was meant to do and destroyed every single magic carpet it could find. The legends say there were not two pieces of thread left woven together in Jaktivar by the end of that terrible day."

"Holy Vulture!" said Etan.

"I know. Magnificent, isn't it?" said the Leader. "Most of the city was wrecked; partly by the weapon itself and partly by the magician's desperate attempts to stop it. In the end, it took the King of Jaktivar, all of his magicians and all of the royal guard to recapture the weapon. They all died doing it.

"Meanwhile, the Azamedians had learned of Jaktivar's plans through their spies in the city. They dispatched the largest force they could muster to Jaktivar, with orders to stop the new weapon at any cost. But they needn't have bothered. They arrived to find the last king of Jaktivar dead and the city in ruins. The Azamedians – soft-hearted fools that they are – were so horrified by the destruction that they laid down their weapons and rescued the survivors. Most of these Jaktivarians eventually settled in Azamed, adding their carpet-weaving knowledge to Azamed's. The weapon – the perfect anti-flying carpet weapon – was never seen or heard of again."

The Leader hit the chisel hard. With a loud crack, the blade broke through the stone seal and slipped several inches into the box.

"Until now," said the Leader.

"Holy Vulture!" said Etan.

"Keep it still," said the Leader.

Etan put both his hands on the edge of the box and held it down on the stone. The Leader laid down the hammer and chisel and picked up a crowbar. Fitting it into the gap, he leaned down hard on it. The lid was fitted tight. The Leader grunted and strained and sweat beaded on his forehead behind his mask. Stone squeaked as the lid moved, painfully slowly, and then leapt out of the box with a loud crack.

"AAAAHH!"

The Leader had been pressing so hard on the chisel that he fell over as the lid gave way, knocking Etan down with him. A cloud of dark dust burst out of the box as the airtight seal was broken. The lid landed on Etan's chest. As he lifted it off, his fingers touched grooves carved into the underside. He turned it over.

"Uh… Sir?"

"Wha… What?" the Leader coughed.

Etan held the lid out so the Leader could see it. The underside was covered with writing scratched into the stone. Unlike the neat inscription on the lid, the symbols here were scrawled with energy and fury. They were written in all directions, straight, diagonal and horizontal, criss-crossing over one another. But as he stared at it, Etan realized that all the lines, even the ones written backwards and upside down, contained the same set of symbols in the same order.

"Is it the same thing written over and over again?" he said.

"It is," said the Leader, taking the lid from him and turning it around. He frowned as he deciphered the ancient High Jaktivarian by memory from the notes he had stolen from Qwinton's study before they left Azamed.

"What does it say?" said Etan.

"*Release me*," said the Leader.

They looked at each other. Then they stood up. Slowly, they both peered into the box.

Etan blinked. The Leader beamed behind his mask.

"At last!" he breathed. "It's perfect!"

"That's it?" said Etan. "That?"

"Yes, it is," said the Leader. "That is our revenge on Azamed."

Stones clattered down the slope from the tunnel behind them. The Leader and Etan looked around as Hara and Mira slipped like panthers back into the cave.

"Oh, good. About time," said the Leader. "Did you get it?"

"There were more guards than we expected, sir, but we did," said Hara. She opened her haversack and drew out an old green glass bottle.

"Excellent!" said the Leader, taking it from her.

The bottle was large and rather crudely made. Tiny air bubbles were trapped inside the dark green glass. It might have once held wine, but now it was old and scratched and sand-scarred, as if it had been buried in the desert for years. The outside of it was so damaged that it was impossible to see what was inside.

"Splendid!" said the Leader. "It's also perfect!"

"Why couldn't we just have hired Miss Storm-strong to steal it, sir?" said Etan.

"Because this part of the plan was too important to entrust to anyone else," said the Leader. "This is our revenge."

"But I thought the box was, sir?"

"No, the box is our revenge on Azamed," said the Leader. "This is our revenge on Zal Thesa and Zara Aura."

By now, it was evening and the sky over Shirazar was a dark shade of purple. Everything was closed apart from the restaurants, and the gardens grew quiet as the butterflies turned in for the night. The moon was rising and the stars were coming out as the Thesas and the Auras hurried through the empty streets with Rip leading the way.

"Are you sure we've got everything?" said Zara. "What about the tassel brush?"

"Yes, for the five-hundredth time! I double checked," said Zal. He was carrying the emergency carpet-cleaning supplies in a large box. "What about the balm? Is that OK?"

"I think so. I've never made any before," said

131

Zara. "Alchemy is not one of my best subjects."

She held up the extra-large glass jar she was carrying. It was filled to the tightly-screwed-on lid with the misty pale blue potion, glowing softly with magic. Before he had gone home to tell his father what was going on, Miles had helped them collect the water from the stream in the museum gardens. When they got back to the hotel, Zal and Rip had paced up and down the length of the suite while Zara had locked herself in her bedroom and worked for the rest of the afternoon. They had heard the whisper of magic being cast, a lot of mumbling, a lot of cursing and several strange smells before she had emerged. Following Professor Maltho's instructions, she had mixed all five ingredients together, infused them with magic and produced the single large jar full of what she *hoped* was Rivertree balm. All they needed now was a proper magic carpet repair frame to try it out.

"Try to relax a little, Zara," said Augur. "I'm sure it will work. You've both worked miracles with carpets before. You can do it again."

"Quite right," said Arna, who was carrying his favourite crossbow and was peering into every corner, every doorway, every side street and every shadow they passed. "It's the Shadows I'm worried about. If they're here, they're bound to be plotting something vile. Sabotaging the Champions' Race is just the sort of diabolical scheme they'd try."

Zal and Zara both nodded. After Qwinton had done the translation, Captain Curta had thanked them for their help, but told them to leave the investigation – and the hunt for the missing box – to him, and then sent them on their way.

"There's no one better than you two when it comes to magic or carpets," said Augur. "If you can't make it work, no one can."

"Just don't sell any of the spares until after we've tried it," said Zal. "If it doesn't work, we need to pick the best one so we can at least ask to race on it instead."

Rip barked and jumped up and down as they arrived in front of a large shop with wide front windows. Inside, dozens of Azamedian carpets glowed in the lamplight. The sign above the door read DENJAR'S CARPET EMPORIUM – LARGEST IN SHIRAZAR. Pinned to the door was a smaller notice that read: CLOSED THIS EVENING FOR SPECIAL RESTOCKING! THE CARPETS

"I think he's expecting us," said Augur.

"Drat! We should have come here last so he'd get desperate and pay more," said Arna. He knocked twice on the door.

"Coming! Coming!" came a voice from inside. The door was opened by a tall and very fat man, in a green robe and blue turban, with a long moustache that drooped down to his waist.

"At last!" he cried. "Augur! Arna! Welcome back, my friends!"

"Denjar! Splendid to see you!" said Arna, shaking his hand. "How's our best Shirazan customer?"

"Wonderful, thank you, and getting better by the minute now you're here," said Denjar. "Hello, Zal. Hello, Rip. And this must be Zara."

"Nice to meet you, Mr Denjar," said Zara.

"The pleasure's all mine. I've lost count of how many times I've heard Zal whining about you," said Denjar. "Now, I imagine you've brought something for me?"

"We have indeed," said Arna. He placed his hand on the block of carpets as Augur steered it forward. "Say hello to the perfect flying carpet!"

"Splendid!" said Denjar. "I've been dreaming about this moment. Bring them in."

Inside, the shop was bright and warm. Hundreds of magic carpets were rolled up and stacked in special shelves. Others were spread out on large display tables or hung from the walls. They were in combinations of all seven colours of magic, but never more than six colours in any one. Signs on the shelves divided the carpets up by weaver, and in front of the Thesa shelf, an empty table was set out with a sign next to it that read: NEW IN! RAINBOW CARPETS! RIDE THE CARPET THAT WON THE GREAT RACE OF AZAMED!

"I take it you'll want several," said Augur.

"Several? Of course not!" said Denjar. "I want all of them. Once it was announced that Zal and Zara were Azamed's Champions this year, every carpet flyer in the city guessed you'd be bringing some to sell. I'm up to my neck in pre-orders already. How many did you bring?" he said, as Zal and Zara set the Rainbow Carpet down on the floor. "Oh, is that another one?"

"It was," said Zara, as she and Zal unrolled it.

"BY THE STORK'S FEET!" Denjar staggered backwards, going white with the horror of a true

135

connoisseur of flying carpets. The ends of his moustache dropped even further. "What happened?"

"Twelve octopuses," said Zal. "And the Crystal Flowers of Kandara. It's a long story."

"Gentle River Robin! It must be!" said Denjar. "What a disaster!"

"But we think we can clean it," said Zara, holding up the jar of Rivertree balm. "Could we possibly use your carpet repair frame? We don't want to risk doing it on the hotel floor."

"Please do!" said Denjar, waving them towards the small workshop in the far corner of the showroom. "Good grief, how terrible! Yes, of course. Anything I can do to help."

"Thank you," said Zara, as Zal carried the carpet to the workshop. As well as selling carpets, Denjar also repaired them for his customers and he had all the tools and equipment needed. Zara set the jar down on a workbench with their box of cleaning supplies while Zal carefully hung the Rainbow Carpet from the frame.

"Use whatever you need," said Denjar. "Now then, Augur. Forty-seven rainbow carpets and the one they're sitting on. How much do you want for all of them?"

"It's very generous of you to let us set the price, Denjar, but we were planning to show them to a few of our other Shirazan customers as well," said Augur. "We are all good friends after all."

"Yes, but we're also all businessmen," said Denjar. "Fifteen thousand gold pieces for the lot."

"Twenty," said Augur and Arna together.

Zal hung the carpet carefully from the repair frame and smoothed it out. He turned around to watch as Zara unscrewed the lid of the jar, being careful not to spill any. She chose a paintbrush from Denjar's tool rack and dipped it in. The balm was thick and smooth like honey.

"We should try it on the tassels first," said Zara. "In case the Professor was right."

"OK," said Zal, looking at the grey and black mess of the carpet's surface. His heart was pounding. This could save them, or it could leave them where they had started, and with less time to go before the race. Rip whimpered and Zal picked him up so he could see.

"Three hundred gold pieces each," said Denjar.

"We're selling them for twice that in Azamed," said Augur.

137

"Very well. Six hundred."

"No."

Gingerly, biting her lower lip, Zara lowered the paintbrush towards the carpet.

"Oh, by the way, Zara," said Arna, reaching into his pocket. "This came earlier for you."

Zara moved the brush away, gritting her teeth, before it dripped on the carpet.

"It did?" she said.

"Yes, a long-distance, high-speed homing pigeon came before you got back," said Arna, pulling out a note. "Sorry, I forgot all about it. It's from Qwinton."

"Qwinton?" said Zal.

"Yes. He says he made a mistake in the translation," said Arna, peering at the note. "It wasn't 'Night Demon' but 'Knife Demon' whatever that means. He says sorry for the mistake and please bring him some Frostbite Yeti Yogurt—"

THUNK!

They all jumped at the sound of wood cracking, split by something stronger than an axe.

"What in the name of...!" Denjar spun around and froze, staring at the shop's door.

A large black dagger had been driven through the

solid wooden door, above the top hinge. The blade was wide, heavy and black as obsidian. Its tip was forked into two points like a snake's tongue.

"Hello?" said Denjar. "We're closed."

The dagger blade moved. It shifted up and down and the hole it had made widened. Then it started moving back and forth, sawing through the wood with ease. Sawdust flew as the dagger cut down as far as the bottom hinge, then turned sideways, sawing across the bottom of the door and then up the other side. Zal watched with astonishment. No one was strong enough to do that.

"What in name of the Stork?" said Augur.

"The Shadows!" said Arna, grabbing his crossbow.

The dagger blade made its final cut across the top of the door, then slid back out of sight. There was a second's pause, then something hit the door with a hard bang. The rough-edged rectangle of the middle of the door flew into the room as the dagger spun in behind it.

"HOLY STORK!" Augur, Arna and Denjar jumped out of its way.

Zal's mouth dropped open. No one – *no one* – could have thrown the dagger hard enough to do that. He stared through the giant hole in what was left of the door, half expecting to see a Quakajakian gorilla outside.

There was nothing. The darkened street was empty. Out of the corner of his eye, Zal suddenly noticed the dagger was still in the air.

Behind its forked blade, the dagger had a snake-shaped hilt, a short oval handle and a heavy round pommel. The handle had no finger grooves and it was not even wrapped in wire to make it easier to grip. The whole dagger was made from one piece of blackened steel. It was hovering two metres above the floor in the middle of the room. Zal watched as it turned slowly around, as if it was taking in the view.

"Knife Demon," said Zara.

The dagger moved. It flew down to the nearest table, curving smoothly through the air, and used its forked tip to cut straight through the beautiful green, pink and orange three-shader that was on display there.

"NO!" shouted Denjar, the ends of his moustache standing bolt upright.

The dagger cut the carpet cleanly in half across the middle, then flew in a tight circle and slashed each piece in half from end to end.

"BY THE STORK!" yelled Arna.

"GOOD GRIEF!" shouted Augur.

"MY MERCHANDISE!" screamed Denjar, as the dagger flew straight to the next table and sliced through three elegant purple single-shaders and then cut through six others on the next table. It rose into the air again and turned its points towards the shelves.

"NO! STOP, YOU FIENDISH THING!"

The dagger flew into the shelves and began carving its way through the rolled carpets. Denjar dived across the room and grabbed a broom. He raced over to the shelves and beat at the dagger with the broom handle. The dagger dodged out of the way and flew in a sharp spiral, cutting the broom handle into four pieces and slicing off Denjar's moustache, leaving him frozen with shock.

Zal leapt over the nearest table and charged forwards, drawing his sword. That was why the handle was not grooved! The dagger was not meant to be held, it was meant to fly! He skidded in front of Denjar and swung his sword. The metal rang and sparks flew as his blade crashed into the dagger, flipping it sideways in the air. Zal pressed forwards, hacking and slashing at it, and though the dagger tried to move out of the way, Zal kept knocking it backwards, away from the shelves and the carpets. The dagger knew how to cut up carpets, but it did not know how to sword fight, especially not against a student of Mistress Shen. Zal beat the dagger sideways, knocked its points down towards the floor and lunged forward, putting all his strength into the blade for the winning stroke, aiming behind the handle for where … the hand holding the dagger would be.

Zal's heart skipped a beat. There was no hand holding the dagger. In the excitement of a real sword fight, he'd forgotten it was moving by itself! His sword curved through empty air, his momentum pulling him with it. His feet skidded on the floorboards and he fell over. He landed on his hands and looked up, just as the dagger flew downwards and hit him on the forehead with its pommel.

"OWW!" Zal collapsed on the floor, stars spinning in front of his eyes.

"ZAL! STAY DOWN!" shouted Zara.

Zara threw out her arms and sent twin red combat

spells spinning across the room. She could feel magic resonating from the dagger, an immensely old and powerful spell. To her horror, her spells hit it and washed straight over it. Her magic broke apart like a raindrop hitting a paving stone. The dagger did not even notice and continued its rampage, flying in a wide circle around the room, cutting through carpets. Zara followed its path, hitting it with a stream of spells in the orange, yellow, green, blue, indigo and violet shades. None of them worked. The dagger was protected against spell casting.

"ZARA! OUT OF THE WAY!" shouted Arna. He raised his crossbow, took aim and fired. The thick arrow shot across the room, hit the dagger and broke into pieces against the blade.

"Oh, camelpat!" Arna dived sideways as the dagger flew across the room in his direction and Augur pulled the distraught Denjar out of the way.

"WRAFF, WRAFF!" Rip sprang onto a chair, then onto a table, jumped and clamped his teeth around the dagger's handle. The dagger slowed and its hilt drooped as Rip's weight pulled it down. The dagger tried flying in a circle, then in a fast figure-of-eight to shake the small dog off, but Rip held on.

"GOOD BOY, RIP!" shouted Zal, pulling himself up on one of the tables with one hand and rubbing his forehead with the other. "HOLD ON... OH, STORK!"

The dagger suddenly nosedived and drove both its points into the floor.

"WRAAAL!" Rip was thrown off by the sudden impact and landed safely in a pile of cut-up six-shaders.

"OH, HOLY STORK!" said Zara, as the dagger wiggled free. It flew straight towards the last carpets left in the room, the block of new rainbow carpets, which it either hadn't noticed before, or had decided to save for last.

"NOOO!" shouted Augur, Arna and Denjar together.

The dagger vanished into the block. They watched in horror as the rolled-up carpets swayed slightly and then started to sink inwards. Cut-up sections of rainbow carpet rolled out of it like ribbons and then the dagger burst triumphantly out of the bottom row, cutting through the last rainbow carpet that the block was floating on.

"ZAL!" Zara screamed.

Zal, staring in horror at the ruined block, followed her gaze and his heart turned to ice. The Rainbow Carpet – *the* Rainbow Carpet, *their* Rainbow Carpet – was still hanging on the repair frame and the dagger was turning towards it.

"NO!!!"

"WRAFF!!!"

Zal, Zara and Rip dived across the room, knocking the frame flat and throwing themselves on top of it and the carpet. They looked up as the dagger appeared above them – and stopped dead in the air.

Everyone froze. There was no sound except panting. The dagger hovered motionless over the black and grey Rainbow Carpet. It tilted sideways, as if it was considering it. Then it turned slowly in the air, surveying the rest of the shop. Sliced carpets were strewn over the tables like torn ribbons, hanging from the shelves and pooling on the floor. Of the hundreds of flying carpets in the shop, the ruined Rainbow Carpet was the only one left intact.

The dagger turned all the way around to face the hole in the door and flew back towards it, over the top of Denjar's workbench, and its hilt caught the rim of the jar of Rivertree balm.

"No!" cried Zara, as the jar rocked and wobbled.

Zal got to his knees and scrambled forwards, but he was too late. The jar overturned, rolled off the table and broke, spilling Rivertree balm all over the floor. The dagger flew out of the door and vanished into the night as Zal and Zara watched in horror as the glowing blue potion soaked into the floorboards.

On the rooftop of a building across the street, the Knife Demon flew straight into the Leader's hand.

"Magnificent!" said the Leader, smiling almost wide enough to tear his scarf. "The unstoppable power of the Knife Demon! It's exactly like the legends said."

"That was amazing!" said Etan, his eyes shining. They had watched the whole thing through the shop's front windows.

"Just wait until we get back home and unleash it for real," said the Leader. "All of Azamed will beg for mercy. That will be a sight worth seeing."

"How soon do we leave, sir?" asked Hara.

"As soon as we have our vengeance on Zal and Zara," said the Leader. "We're going home once we've made sure that they never will."

"Let me do it now, sir," said Mira, drawing her scimitar. The curved blade gleamed in the moonlight. "They'll still be in shock in there."

"No, a slow and painful death by the sword is far too good for them," said the Leader. "We'll stick with the plan. It will give them a far more nightmarish fate and … OWW!"

The Leader jumped as the Knife Demon jabbed its points into one of his fingers. It flew out of his hand and down to the roof tiles at their feet.

"What?" said the Leader.

The Knife Demon pressed its points into the roof. Metal shrieked on terracotta and red dust flew as it moved back and forth.

MORE CARPETS! it carved into the roof tiles.

Seven

"I don't understand," said Miles. "Why didn't it go for the Rainbow Carpet?"

It was half an hour later. Zal and Zara were sitting in the kitchen of the Nocturne family home, clutching hot cups of tea and still shaking. Rip was ravenously helping himself to Fluffy's bowl in the corner and Fluffy was watching without complaining.

"Because it's not a rainbow carpet any more," said Zara. "The Knife Demon must be enchanted to go after the seven colours, but because black isn't one of them, it left the carpet alone."

"Or it just didn't bother with it," said Zal.

The Nocturne home was large and comfortable.

Every room seemed to have a telescope in it made by Miles' grandmother. In the garden, right beside the giant birdhouse that Celeste roosted in, there was a large pond with a family of water dragons living in it. As the house was closer to Denjar's shop than the hotel, Zal and Zara had come here to recover from what had just happened.

"So as long it's covered in ink and can't fly, it's safe, but as soon as you fix it, the Knife Demon will go straight for it?" said Miles. "Camelpat! What a twist of fate."

"Don't worry. We can't fix it until we get more Rivertree balm," said Zal.

"There's no point," said Zara. "It won't work."

She drew out a roughly cut strip of carpet and laid it on the table. It looked like one of the hundreds the Knife Demon had left strewn about the shop in its wake, but it was white. Zal blinked, trying to remember if he had seen a white carpet in Denjar's shop. Then he noticed that there were four different weaving patterns running through it.

"It was a four-shader," said Zara. "The Rivertree balm soaked it when the jar broke. The Professor was right. It washed the dye out of the threads."

"Oh, Stork!" said Zal. "Now we're finished. For real this time!"

"What about the Knife Demon?" said Miles. "Are you absolutely sure there's no way to stop it?"

"How?" said Zal. "It moves by itself and there's no one holding it to attack. We tried swords and magic. Nothing worked."

"I tried all seven colours," said Zara, shivering again. "It was unstoppable."

"Holy Stork!" said Miles. "It's the perfect weapon to sabotage the Champions' Race! I wish I'd known about it sooner… I mean, maybe we could have stopped them getting it. Oh, I wish Dad was here so I could warn him."

"Where is Paradim anyway?" said Zal.

"He and Celeste went for a night-time training flight," said Miles. "Celeste was hatched in Frostbite, remember? She likes flying at night when it's cold. I don't understand why. I can't stand cold weather."

"You couldn't have stopped the Shadows if they really wanted it," said Zal.

"I learnt that this afternoon," said Miles. "The sergeants came in to report while Captain Curta was telling me off for bringing you there. They'd been

150

all over the museum and the gardens twice and the headscarf was the only clue anyone found. The only other thing that wasn't meant to be there was a couple of tiger tracks in one of the flowerbeds."

"What?" said Zal, looking up. "Tiger tracks?"

"Yes. Three full-sized paw prints," said Miles.

"What is it?" said Zara, looking at Zal.

"Tiger tracks?" said Zal, staring straight ahead. "At the Academy, Professor Maltho said that when the Crystal Flowers were stolen, the only clue they found was some black and orange fur in the display case."

"What?" said Miles. "Tiger fur?"

"And now tiger tracks at the museum," said Zal. "After the Knife Demon was stolen... That means..."

"OH, HOLY STORK!" said Miles.

He and Zal stood bolt upright, spilling their tea. Their faces went white as they pointed at each other with horror.

"Sari Stormstrong!" they said together.

"Who the Stork is Sari Stormstrong?" said Zara, five minutes later, as Zal finished checking all the doors were locked.

"She's the most notorious thief in the Great Desert," said Miles, peering out through the kitchen window. He had just dashed back downstairs from checking that his father's trophy cabinet was still where it was meant to be. "She stole the Caldyn Prophecy Stones, the Diamond Crown of Endsali, the original copy of the Poems of Dalvina and pretty much everything else that's worth stealing in the Seventeen Kingdoms."

"She's an orphan," said Zal. "She was raised by tigers in the Quakajakian Rainforest and now she uses trained tigers in her burglaries. There's a whole wall of WANTED posters for her in the Caliph's Guard Offices at home. They put them up after she stole the Caliph's wife's favourite water lilies."

"Only one wall?" said Miles. "There are three in the Royal Protectors' Headquarters. But then again, she's … 'worked' in Shirazar way more times than she's been in Azamed. Camelpat! I can't believe I didn't see this before! She's the perfect suspect for the crime wave."

"But hold on, the Shadows are behind the crime wave," said Zara. "We know they are. We found that headscarf at the museum."

"No, that's what I mean," said Miles. "The

Shadows are Azamedians. Lord Dasat was right. They'd find it hard to pull off so many burglaries here. So they'd need someone who knows Shirazar. Sari Stormstrong would be perfect."

"She is a mercenary thief," said Zal. "She doesn't steal for herself. People hire her to steal stuff for them. The Shadows must have hired her to help them steal the Knife Demon."

"And everything else that they're going to need to sabotage the Champions' Race," said Miles. "Well done, Zal. You're a genius."

"Oh, thanks."

"Let's just hope Captain Curta can see it too," said Miles. He grabbed a warm outdoor robe from a peg by the door and pulled it on.

"Where are you going?" said Zara.

"As a Royal Protector Cadet, it's my duty to inform my superior officers immediately if I think there might be an internationally wanted criminal in the city," said Miles. "If I can get the Captain to believe us, he'll order an immediate search."

"That would help," said Zal. "Maybe if we can find her, she can take us to the Shadows before they use the Knife Demon again."

"Exactly," said Miles. "But you two better wait here. He threatened to court martial me if I tried to smuggle foreign visitors into a Shirazan investigation again."

"Hold on, could you really find her quickly?" said Zara. "I know this is my first visit, but Shirazar's a big place."

"It is, but if Sari Stormstrong is here, she'll probably be staying in one of few places," said Miles. "The Desert Crab, most likely."

"The what?" said Zal.

"It's a disreputable inn on Plateau's Edge Street," said Miles. "All the smugglers who come to Shirazar from the Deep Desert stay there."

"Where is it again?" said Zara, standing up.

"Whoa! Hold on!" said Miles, holding up his hands. "You can't go there. It's dangerous. It's the most lawless corner of Shirazar."

"Yes, but what's the address?" said Zal.

"Zal, I'm serious," said Miles. "You can get more than your wallet stolen around there. They'd probably even steal your hair to sell it on the underground wig market. Let me get Captain Curta. Then we can do this safely."

"OK," said Zal.

"If that's what you think is best," said Zara.

"Hold on," said Miles, his eyes narrowing at their easy agreement. "Promise me you *won't* go there alone."

"Sure."

"No problem."

As its name suggested, Plateau's Edge Street ran around the rim of the Shirazar Plateau. Most of the houses there did not have back gardens, just doors that opened straight over the rocky drop down to the desert. Cold winds rose up the cliffs from the sands, moaning like ghosts and swinging the creaky sign above the Desert Crab's entrance. The inn was a large, ramshackle building that looked like it had been jumbled together out of rooms stolen from various other inns. The curtains were always drawn across the windows, even in the middle of the day. Tiles were missing from the roof, but the gutters and drainpipes were fixed firmly to the walls in case the inn's customers needed to climb down them when the Royal Protectors paid a visit. There were several back doors and more than one cellar. The main room was busy and the big fireplace was blazing when Zal and Zara walked in.

"Holy Stork!" said Zal, under his breath. He quickly checked his sword and his wallet.

Bandits, brigands, river pirates, footpads, camel rustlers, sheep smugglers and every other kind of Great Desert criminal, mostly with dark eyes and thick beards that could be shaved off quickly when they needed to change their identities, were sitting in close circles around their tables. They were laughing and talking loudly to one another, but eyeing the other groups with suspicion and keeping their hands on the hilts of their knives. Rip whimpered behind Zal's ankles, looking at the huge hunting dogs that were sprawled around the room, chewing on bones bigger than he was.

"Just look tough," whispered Zara. "Act like we belong here."

"Maybe we should have waited for Miles."

"We said we wouldn't come here alone and we didn't. We came together," said Zara. "Come on."

Zara walked confidently across the room and up to the bar, where the innkeeper was pouring a drink for an ivory smuggler.

"Hello there," said Zara. "We're looking for Sari Stormstrong."

"Never heard of her," said the innkeeper. "Isn't it past your bedtime?"

"I don't think you heard me correctly," said Zara, dropping a handful of silver pieces on the bar. "I said we're looking for Sari Stormstrong."

"Oh, *Sari Stormstrong*!" said the innkeeper, sweeping the coins into his hand and putting them in the pocket of his apron. "Why didn't you say so in the first place? Upstairs in the booths."

"Thanks very much," said Zara, as she and Zal headed for the stairs.

The first floor was quieter. The only sounds were the whispered conversations coming from inside the booths that lined the walls and the clink of money changing hands.

"Now how do we find her?" whispered Zal. Peering into each booth in turn was probably not going to be the safest option.

"You're the criminal expert," said Zara. "How would… Wait! Zal, look!"

Across the room, three waitresses who looked like the innkeeper's daughters, were walking towards a booth at the far end. They were each carrying two large trays of raw meat.

"I think we've found her," said Zara.

They approached the booth. Zal tried to keep his face tough as they looked around the wooden partition, but his eyes still widened slightly at the sight of the three full-grown tigers lying on the benches inside it, eating meat from the trays. Their orange fur glowed and shimmered in the lamplight, as they looked up at him and Zara with lazy curiosity. Rip hid behind Zal's ankles again. Sitting in the middle of the tigers, with her back to the wall, was a tall girl dressed in green, eating a large bowl of rice and stew. Zal had never seen her before, but he recognized the long black ponytail and the four thin scars on her cheek straight away from a dozen WANTED posters.

"Sari Stormstrong?" said Zara.

"Who wants to know?" said the girl.

"I'm Zahna Aurada," said Zara, sitting down beside Jeweltail. "This is my cousin, Zarl Thessalay."

"Hello," said Zal. He sat down on the opposite bench beside Cloudclaw, who growled and bared his teeth. Zal quickly stood up again.

158

"We hear you can steal anything," said Zara.

"You've got good ears," said Sari, eating another mouthful of stew.

"Does anything include information?" said Zara.

"Sometimes."

"Good. Then we want to hire you," said Zara. "There was a theft at the Shirazar Museum last night; an ancient stone casket. It contains something very old, rare and valuable. Our uncles are black magicians and they had plans for it, so we need to get it back. We'll pay you three thousand gold pieces if you can find out who stole it and four thousand if you can find out where they are."

"Twelve thousand," said Sari.

"Four," said Zara.

"Twelve."

"Four."

"I don't work for less than twelve," said Sari.

"That's good because this isn't work," said Zara. "We're hiring you to ask around for us, not to do anything difficult or dangerous. Three thousand if you can find who the thieves are and four if you can get their address."

Sari looked at Zara for a moment, chewing

thoughtfully. The tigers watched her. Zal and Rip waited.

"OK. We have a deal," said Sari. "Four thousand it is. I'll find out who it was and where they are. Don't worry, you don't have to pay me in advance."

"Great," said Zara, as Sari stood up. "How long is this going to take?"

"About five minutes," said Sari, as the tigers flowed off the benches. Zal and Rip jumped out of the way. "Come on."

"Where are we going?" said Zal.

"Upstairs," said Sari, with a smile. "The best information trader in Shirazar lives on the top floor."

"Couldn't you have mentioned the trader earlier?" said Zara, as they followed Sari up the narrow backstairs of the inn.

"Sure," said Sari. "But why would I? You'd have paid less."

"We still might," said Zal. He was walking behind the tigers, trying very carefully not to step on their tails and carrying Rip, who had refused point blank to walk on the floor with them.

"Too late. A deal's a deal," said Sari. "Now be quiet."

She led them along a narrow corridor under the inn's roof. The doors were all numbered and Sari stopped outside number thirteen. She knocked three times, paused and then knocked twice more. She listened and then nodded to Zal and Zara. She took out a key, unlocked the door and opened it and motioned for them to go in.

"Good evening," said Zara, as they walked in. "My name is…"

She stopped as she saw the room was empty. The tiny bedroom had a wardrobe, a table and chair, a washbasin and one unmade bed.

"Where's the…?" said Zara, as Sari pushed Zal inside and kicked the door shut behind her. Her tigers lowered their heads and growled. Sari picked up a spear that was standing in the corner.

"I stole the box from the museum," said Sari, "and I'm standing right here. That'll be four thousand gold pieces."

Everyone moved at once. Zal's sword shot out of his scabbard and knocked the head of Sari's spear aside as she stabbed at his stomach. Zara jumped backwards, filling her hands with magic, just as the tigers slammed into her. Zara cursed as she landed hard on the floor with Cloudclaw, Jeweltail and Sheertooth pinning her arms and making sure they were pointed away from Sari. She struggled, but the tigers were too heavy.

"WRROOOOAAAR!" Cloudclaw suddenly leapt into the air, roaring with pain and knocking his brother and sister off. Zara slid across the floor underneath him, unsure what had happened, and saw Rip flying through the air, hanging onto Cloudclaw's tail by his teeth.

"Good boy!" Zal shouted over his shoulder, as he fenced against Sari's spear. She was a very good fighter, wielding the weapon that was far too long for the small room with speed and skill. Zal whipped his sword back and forth, keeping the point at bay.

"GGGRRR*AARGH!*"

Sheertooth skidded backwards with his fur smoking as Zara hit him with a spell. She dropped to one knee and ducked as Jeweltail lunged for her again, sailing over her head and landing on the bed. Zara quickly threw out a green spell, aiming not at the tiger, but at the blankets. The bedclothes rose up like waves in the sea and wrapped around Jeweltail, trapping the struggling tiger on the bed.

Cloudclaw, thrashing and roaring with rage, finally shook Rip off. Rip landed on his paws and scurried straight under the bed. Cloudclaw surged after him, but his head was too large to follow. As he tried, Sheertooth collided with him as he charged back at Zara. Zara jumped out of the way as they rolled past in a tangle of legs and paws. Zal knocked Sari's spear point aside and lunged forward, but she kicked him in the chest with her heel and drove him back beside Zara. Sheertooth and Cloudclaw rushed to Sari's side as Jeweltail tore her way out of the blankets. Rip peeped out from under the bed. The two sides faced one another across the room.

"OK," said Zal, panting. "We know it was you."

"Really?" said Sari. "Maybe you're not as stupid as you look."

"But we also know someone hired you to steal it," said Zara. "You're not important. You're just a thief-for-hire. All you care about is where your next payment is coming from."

Sari's green eyes darkened even more, but she didn't say anything.

"We're interested in the people who hired you," said Zara. "If you tell us where to find them, we'll still pay you."

"Yes. Our fathers need the casket," said Zal.

"Our uncles, Zarl."

"Don't bother with the stupid fake names, Azamedians. I know who you are," said Sari, glancing at the door. "OK, city-dwellers, we have a deal – a new one. I won't just tell you where they are; I'll take you straight to them. But we need to leave right now."

"Why?" said Zal.

From somewhere downstairs, they heard a door crashing open.

"ROYAL PROTECTORS! NOBODY MOVE! WE HAVE A WARRANT TO SEARCH THESE PREMISES FOR AN INTERNATIONALLY WANTED THIEF!"

"Oh, camelpat," said Zal.

"You'd better be able to keep up," said Sari, opening the room's window and letting cold air rush in. "Don't worry. They're not far."

"Wraff, wraff!"

"Squeak! Squeak! Squeak!"

Water dripped from stalactites as Rip chased several rats along the tunnel. Cloudclaw watched him and growled, swishing his still-crumpled tail.

"How long have they been hiding down here?" whispered Zara, trying not to slip on the wet moss that covered the rocky floor.

"How should I know?" said Sari. "I respect my clients' privacy. That way, I get more clients."

"Why did you take us upstairs if you knew who we were?" said Zal.

"Why did you come upstairs to find out who the thief was if you knew it was me?" said Sari. "I just wanted to see if you were really that stupid."

"We came because we wanted to know where the Shadows are. We don't care about you," said Zal.

"Shsssh!" said Zara, holding up her hand. "Listen."

Zal and Rip froze. Sari rolled her eyes. From further down the tunnel, voices drifted towards them.

"What do you think, sir? Should we do it?"

"I'm not sure, Hara. I'm just not sure. It would certainly be entertaining..."

Zal and Zara crept forward. Zal wrapped his fingers around his sword hilt. Red magic glowed in Zara's hands. Around the next turning, the tunnel ended in a ledge that overlooked a large cave. The orange light of a campfire glowed on the ceiling.

"But there are thousands of Azamedian spectators here in Shirazar right now. If we do let our demonic piece of cutlery loose on the Champions' Race—"

"Oh! Word might get back to Azamed before we do, sir?"

"Don't interrupt, Etan."

Zal and Zara slid forward on their stomachs and peered over the ledge. Below them, sleeping bags and haversacks were set out around the campfire. A cooking pot was boiling above it. Four Shadows were present, two women – Zal and Zara both blinked, having never seen a female Shadow before – and a boy sat near one young man, who was reclining against a comfortable, chair-shaped rock. Zal shivered. He had known they were back, but seeing them and their brown uniforms again was still enough to make his blood run cold. But the Shadows had not noticed them. All four were completely distracted. He and Zara looked at each other and nodded. They were never going to get a better chance than this.

"One," whispered Zara. "Two. Three!"

She and Zal sprang to their feet. Zal's sword rang against the lip of his scabbard and the warmth of combat magic filled Zara's hands.

THWACK!

"AAAAAHH!!!"

Something hard had come from nowhere and struck the back of Zal's head. He plunged forward over the stone ledge, losing his grip on his sword and landing on his front on the cold stone floor. As he gasped in pain, Zara landed beside him, having been hit as she tried to turn around.

"What the Vulture!" yelled the Leader, falling backwards over his stone chair.

"Holy Cosmos Vulture! It's them!" cried Etan.

Hara and Mira leapt to their feet, drawing their swords. Zal lunged forward across the ground, reaching for his.

"GRRRR!"

"OOOMPH!"

Before Zal could grab hold of his sword, Sheertooth landed on top of him, pinning him down with heavy paws. Zara cried out as Jeweltail landed on her, breaking her concentration as she tried to form new spells. She pulled one arm free and pointed it at the Shadows, just before Etan leapt in front of her, holding out a metal talisman on a long chain. He quickly looped it over Zara's head.

"WAAAAAHH!"

The magic vanished from Zara's hand. She felt like she had been wrapped in a dozen blankets soaked in freezing bath water. Her skin crawled away from the cold and the blazing fire of her magic was suddenly only smouldering inside her. It was a spell-suppression talisman, enchanted to stop her using her magic.

"Wraff, wraff, wraff!" Rip barked and struggled as Cloudclaw picked him up by the scruff of his neck. Sari strode up onto the ledge beside him.

"MISS STORMSTRONG?!" said the Leader.

"Hi, Mr Leader," said Sari. "Sorry to barge in. But I remembered how much you said you wanted revenge on these two."

"You camelpat!" yelled Zal, struggling under Sheertooth. "You sold us out! We had a deal!"

"You don't need to thank me, Mr Leader," said Sari, jumping down from the ledge into the cave.

"A small delivery fee will be just fine. Let's say …
twelve thousand gold pieces?"

The Leader's eyes moved slowly from Zal to Zara
to Rip and then to Sari. They were stretched wide
with horror.

"You … brought … them … to me?" he said.
"NOOOOOOOOOOOOOOOOOOOOOOO!!!"

The Leader fell to his knees, clasping his head
with both hands. His eyes behind his mask were
filled with anguish.

"Sir!" Hara and Mira rushed to his side.

"How could you?!" the Leader shouted at Sari.
"This completely ruins my own plans for revenge!"

"It does?" said Sari. "Oh. Sorry."

"I needed surprise!" said the Leader. "I needed
to spring out of nowhere and tear them limb from
limb! I wanted to leave them as smears on the pavement with their last thought being that they had not
defeated the Shadow Society!"

"We've known you were here since this morning!" said Zara, struggling under Jeweltail.

"You have?" said the Leader. "NOOOOO! Miss
Stormstrong! You Vulture-cursed mercenary! You've
spoiled everything!"

"Sorry. I was just trying to be helpful," said Sari. "So there isn't a finder's fee?"

"No, by Salladan's slippers, there isn't!" said the Leader. "You've ruined a plan for vengeance I've spent six months working out to the tiniest detail! I spent hours choosing between the most gruesome methods of death! I'm not paying you a single bronze piece for this!"

"Oh, well. You win some, you lose some," said Sari. She rested her spear over her shoulder. "They're here now. You can do whatever you want to them. Come on, Cloud, Jewel, Sheer. Let's go."

"Not so fast, my dear!" said the Leader. "I was planning to leave this until later. But you are a loose end my plan can do without."

Hara and Mira raised their swords. Sheertooth and Jeweltail roared, almost shaking the cave, and sprang at them, releasing Zal and Zara. Cloudclaw dropped Rip and charged. Hara and Mira ran forwards and leapt into the air, meeting the tigers with acrobatic jump kicks, knocking their teeth and claws aside. They had learnt from their last encounter.

"Leave them alone!" shouted Sari. She ran forwards, jammed the end of her spear against a rock and pole-vaulted through the air, kicking Hara in the chest with both feet.

"Etan! Kill Miss Stormstrong!" shouted the Leader, digging through one of the packs.

"Trying, sir!" said Etan, struggling to fit an arrow into his crossbow. "Waaah!" he added, as Hara flew backwards from Sari's kick and crashed into him.

Zal scrambled across the floor and grabbed his sword. Zara was trying to pull off the spell-suppression talisman, which Etan had been smart enough to wrap twice around her neck. Zal scurried towards her across the cave.

"Wraff, wraff!" Rip skidded up beside him as they reached Zara, just as she had the talisman half untangled.

"Let's get out of here!" said Zal, as Sari fenced with her spear against Hara and Mira's swords.

"Great idea!" said Zara. They turned around and ran for the tunnel ledge.

"NOT SO FAST!" yelled the Leader.

He threw the pack aside and turned around, pointing an old green glass bottle towards them. It was a secret heirloom of one of the oldest, richest families in Shirazar, which they had kept hidden for generations, knowing how dangerous it was. The Shadow Society had learnt of it one night when the head of the family had been drunk in a tavern during a visit to Azamed.

"Hara! Mira! Get back here!" the Leader shouted. He grabbed Etan by his collar and pulled him beside him. "She can share their fate!"

Hara and Mira backflipped away from Sari and the tigers and landed at the Leader's side. Zal and Zara ran towards the tunnel as Sari and the tigers ran towards the Shadows, just as the Leader pulled the cork out of the bottle.

A whirlwind of sand spewed from the mouth of the bottle. It formed a giant spinning cone of dust that filled the cave like a horizontal tornado. Sari yelled and shielded her face with her forearm. Zal cursed as the grains bit the back of his neck and Zara felt magic, a powerful spell like a heartbeat echoing from deep in the depths of an ocean. Rip yowled and the tigers roared as the sandstorm enveloped them.

"Yes! It works!" cried the Leader.

The whirlwind suddenly changed direction. The sand that had been swirling out of the bottle started swirling back in. Zal was lifted up off his feet and carried backwards through the sandstorm. Rip flew past him, barking with terror, followed by two of the tigers, tumbling heads over tails. Zal flailed, trying to find something to grab on to, but the sand flowed between his fingers.

"HA, HA! AT LAST!" shouted the Leader. "VENGEANCE IS MINE!"

Zara felt the ancient spell echo again, pulsing with energy. This time, she recognized the shades. Indigo, violet and blue were mixed together in it and she realized it was a powerful shrinking spell. The cave faded away and then there was nothing but swirling sands as they were sucked backwards into the bottle.

Eight

"YAAAAAAAAAAAAAAAAAAAAAAAAAA
AAAAAAAAH ... OOOOMMMPH!"

Zal fell head first out of the storm and landed
with a thump on top of a low sand dune. He raised
his head, blinking dust from his eyes, and looked
around. Somehow, he was outside. He was lying
in the desert under an open sky, in the ruins of an
ancient palace. Crumbling stone walls rose out of
the sand and fallen columns and broken statues lay
half buried on the ground around him. A ghostly
wind whistled through the ruins, blowing the loose
sand around in small whirlwinds. The roof had fallen
in long ago and overhead the sky was a strange dark
shade of green that he had never seen before. It was

174

night time and everything was dark and shadowed.

"Zal?"

"Zara?"

Zal twisted his head around and saw Zara ten feet from him, picking herself up beside an old, broken fountain. Its cracked stone bowls were filled with sand.

"Are you…?"

"Yes, I'm OK."

"Where the Stork are we?" said Sari, who just walked up behind him.

"YOU!" Zal's sword was lying beside him on the dune. He grabbed it and rolled over. "You total camelpat! You sold us out… OWW!"

He broke off as Sari jabbed him in the nose with the end of her spear.

"Oh, like you weren't going to turn me over to the Royal Protectors?" said Sari. "Anyway, what is this place?"

"I don't know," said Zara, dusting herself off. "All I know is it's your fault we're here."

"You're the one who wanted to find Mr Leader," said Sari. "Come on, Cloud. Let's go… Cloud? CLOUD!"

Sari looked round. Arched doorways and gaps in the walls led off what must have been some kind of courtyard with the fountain at its centre. There was no sign of the tigers.

"CLOUDCLAW!" shouted Sari, spinning in a circle and gripping her spear. "SHEERTOOTH! JEWELTAIL! WHERE ARE YOU?!"

"They're not here," said Zara, frowning at Sari's spear. It was an amazing coincidence that it had landed right beside her, just as Zal's sword had fallen beside him, or that they had all landed in the same place after being swept through the whirlwind. Zara looked down and found the spell-suppression talisman was glinting on the sand between her feet.

"Wait a minute," said Zal, looking around. "Where's Rip? Rip! RIP! WHERE ARE YOU, BOY?"

They listened as his shouts echoed away across the ruins. There was no answer.

"Oh, monkey droppings!" said Sari, gripping her spear. She started towards the nearest doorway.

"Where are you going?" said Zal.

"Where do you think?" said Sari. "They could be hurt. I've got to find them."

"No, I mean where are you going?" said Zal,

grabbing her shoulder. "We don't know where we are or where they are. We need to stay togeth— OUCH!"

He fell over as Sari spun around and punched him on the nose.

"Do not touch me!" said Sari. "I do not need help from city-dwellers to find my family!"

"Your family?" said Zara. "Look, Zal's right. We should stay together."

"Forget it!"

"Grrrr!"

They stopped and looked around. Standing in the nearest doorway was a giant ape. It was nearly eight feet tall, with wide shoulders and a huge, barrel-shaped chest, covered in shaggy grey fur. Long muscles coiled along its arms. Its forehead furrowed as it peered at them from beneath thick busy eyebrows.

"Oh, Stork," whispered Zal. He reached for his sword.

"Wait!" said Zara. "It might not be—"

"GGGGRRRRAAAAAWWWAAARRRR!" roared the ape, showing two rows of sharp teeth. Its breath was hot enough to make the air ripple.

"Never mind!"

"OOK OOK OOK!"

The ape threw back its head and hooted, beating its chest with its fist and dancing on its flat feet. Answering hoots rose out of the ruins all around them.

"OOK OOK! OOK OOK!"

Two more apes loped into the doorway, carrying clubs made out of giant bones.

"RUN!" shouted Zal.

Elsewhere in the ruins, a mound of sand moved. It shifted from side to side, rose up and down, turned around in a circle and then burst apart as Rip finally dug himself out.

"Wraff!"

The small dog flopped down on the sand, breathing hard. He could not remember what had happened after the Shadow man had uncorked the bottle, but it had not been pleasant. He stood up on shaky legs and looked around. He was in a long, rectangular room without a roof under a strange green sky. It was filled with fallen square columns lying on their sides or leaning against one another, like the wooden blocks he used to help Zal play with when they were both puppies.

"WRAFF, WRAFF!"

Rip barked as loud as he could. He listened as the sound bounced away through the ruins. No one barked back.

Rip lowered his nose to the ground and breathed in. A storm of scents flowed up his nostrils. Sand, night, wind, dust, fire, ashes, charcoal and rubble. But there was no trace of Zal's distinctive odour of hot spiced camel steaks mixed with sword polish or Zara's pleasant aroma of flowers and magic.

Rip scampered forwards, keeping his nose pressed to the ground. He wove through the columns towards the room's arched doorway and then stopped as he found a scent he recognized, a combination of raw meat, claws, tails and fur. He could not place it exactly, but he knew he had smelt it recently and the trail was fresh and strong. Rip followed it out of the room and into a long corridor.

"Grrrrr?"

Rip stopped and looked up slowly into the face of Cloudclaw who was standing right in front of him, their noses inches apart. The other two horribly large cats were standing behind Cloudclaw. Rip felt his fur stand up by itself.

"GRRRAAARR!" said Cloudclaw, as he sprang at him.

"WRAFF, WRAFF!"

Rip ran underneath Cloudclaw while he was airborne and shot between Sheertooth and Jeweltail, who stared at him in surprise. Cloudclaw skidded around in a spray of sand and was after him in an instant.

"WRAFF, WRAFF, WRAFF!"

Rip raced through the ruins, barking for help, squirming under the columns and around the broken statues. Right behind him, Cloudclaw bounded over the obstacles, snarling with fury. Sheertooth and Jeweltail followed him, both hissing at their brother to stop wasting time. Up ahead, Rip saw another doorway and ran straight through it.

"Ook?"

Rip stopped. His heart froze as he realized he might just have made a mistake.

"GGGRAAAARRR!"

Cloudclaw charged into the room behind him, teeth and claws first … and stopped in his tracks. Sitting in a close circle around a campfire, cradling clubs made from giant bones, were seven of the largest, greyest, furriest monkeys Rip had ever seen. They stared back at him and Cloudclaw with wide, surprised eyes as Sheertooth and Jeweltail dashed through the door behind them.

"Wraff?" said Rip, hopefully.

"OOK OOK OOK!"

The apes swarmed to their feet, grabbing their clubs.

"OOK OOK OOK! GAAHK GAAHK GAAHK!"

"ZARA!"

"I'M TRYING!"

Zal, Zara and Sari ran flat out through the ruins, dodging blocks of stone and leaping over fallen statues. Zara glimpsed other things as they raced through the rooms and corridors. Their feet crunched over crumbling scrolls from ancient libraries, broken cups and plates from great dining halls, fragments of mirrors from huge ballrooms and shards of amphoras and cooking pots from kitchens. When it was new the palace must have been the size of a city.

"OOK OOK ! GAAHK GAAHK!"

Eleven apes were barrelling through the ruins behind them, jabbering and hooting as they loped along on their feet and knuckles, carrying their bone clubs. Others were appearing out of the ruins to join the chase. Zal's sword blade was chipped and Sari was carrying the top half of her broken spear from when they had tried to fight them off.

Zara threw back her arm and tried again, focusing on the burning red shade of magic inside her. She sent her power down her arm and into her hand, trying to send it out through her palm in the form of an ape-repelling combat spell. But nothing happened. Her magic filled her palm, glowing underneath her skin and stopped there. Zara pushed and groaned through her teeth. Her magic wouldn't budge. Something was working against her. It wasn't Etan's spell-suppression talisman this time; that was wrapped up in her pocket in case it came in handy. Something else was lying over everything in the ruins, stopping her from using her powers.

"Zara?!"

"It's no good!" said Zara. "I can't do it!"

"Well, do something!" said Sari. She stooped while she was running, picked up a rock and threw it over her shoulder at the apes. It bounced off the leading ape's head, making it roar and lope even faster.

"Stop doing that!" said Zara.

"Wait! This way!" said Zal.

Zal darted through the door to another room. Zara and Sari followed him. The room might once have been a kitchen. It was long with what looked like deep oven pits sunk into the floor. There were no other doors.

"What are you doing?" cried Sari, as the apes tried to charge through the doorway behind them and got stuck. The chase slowed down for a few seconds while the apes fought over who would go first, giving Zal the time to run to the far end of the room.

"Here!" he said.

There was a large crack running down the wall from the top to the floor. It was just wide enough for them, standing sideways, to squeeze through.

"Come on!" said Zal, wiggling into the gap.

"Go faster then!" said Sari.

"OWW!" said Zal, as Sari kicked him through and then slipped effortlessly through it herself. Zara squeezed into the gap behind her, just as the apes thundered down the room. Zal and Sari grabbed her from the other side and pulled her clear.

The apes howled with rage. Four grey furry arms

shot through the crack and waved about, grabbing at handfuls of thin air. Fists pounded on the wall on the other side, sending dust flying.

"Phew!" said Zal.

"Come on," said Sari. "They'll find another way around."

They ran again, passing through several more rooms, filled with so much sand that it was impossible to guess what they might have been used for. The apes' howling faded into the distance behind them, but tiredness started to catch up. Zara felt her heart pounding. They slowed and stopped in one of the corridors.

"Where the Stork are we?" said Zal.

"I don't know," said Zara. She leaned one hand against the wall to rest. "I…"

The wall was covered in thick dust, which fell away under Zara's hand and her fingers touched carved grooves. Zara lifted her hand away, leaving a perfect hand print in the dust, and saw the wall was covered in writing. Dozens of sentences were written across it, crossing over one another in all directions.

"What is it?" said Zal.

"I don't know."

Zara brushed off more dust, revealing more sentences. There had to be hundreds of them, written in Shirazan, Azamedian, Jaktivarian, Pursolonian, Yamarotoan, Tabarasari, Hothathian and a dozen other alphabets Zara couldn't recognize. Zara looked more closely at the writing, focusing on the sentences in Azamedian. They were jumbled and some of them were written backwards or upside down, but they all began with the same two words:

I WISH…

"Oh, no!" said Zara, going pale. "Oh, Stork!"

"What is it?" said Zal.

"We're inside a genie bottle!"

"GGGGRRRRR!"

"OOK OOK! *AAAHHK!*"

Cries rang out and sand flew as the tigers and the apes fell on each other. Rip scurried between thick furry legs and broad stamping feet. The campfire flared in a shower of sparks as one of the apes stood in it, trying to grab Sheertooth. Rip skidded around it, trying desperately to find a way out.

"GGGGRRRAAARRRR!"

Behind him, Cloudclaw bit an ape's ankles and slipped out of the way as it tried to grab him. Sheertooth and Jeweltail were clinging to the backs of two apes with their claws and biting their heads and shoulders as the ape's flailed around trying to pull them off. Rip skidded along the edge of the wall and his heart sank. The space they had run into was one of the few intact rooms left in the palace. The four walls were still standing and there was no other door.

"OOK!"

"WRAFF!"

THUD!

Rip dodged just in time as one of the apes swung its club at him. The head of the huge thigh bone hit the wall just above the ground, and smashed a rough hole straight through it.

"AAARGH!" said the ape in frustration.

"Wraff, wraff!" Rip barked in thanks as he jumped through it.

He came out into a more open part of the ruins. Broken walls and columns stretched away before him. The huge monkeys would never fit through the hole. He was safe.

"GGGRRRAAAAARRR!"

Rip looked back through the hole at Jeweltail's cry of pain. One of the apes had just pulled her off the back of its friend, and thrown her against the wall. More were chasing Cloudclaw around the squashed campfire, grunting but ignoring the pain when he clawed or bit them. Three others had cornered Sheertooth against the side wall and were closing in with their clubs raised.

Rip hesitated. They had tried to eat him.

"GGRRRAAAIHHK!"

Jeweltail shrieked as one of the apes grabbed her by her tail. It started pulling her towards him, hand over hand like Zal's father winding up carpet thread. Jeweltail's paws scrabbled at the sand, trying to grip it with her claws. Tears beaded in her eyes as she hissed with pain.

"WRAFF, WRAFF!" Rip jumped barking back into the room.

"GRROOAAARR!" Before he could reach Jeweltail, Sheertooth broke free of the apes surrounding him. He flew across the room and landed on the monkey pulling his sister. The ape hooted as Sheertooth knocked it and its two friends over.

187

Jeweltail broke free, her tail badly ruffled, and joined Cloudclaw in bolting about the room.

"WRAFF, WRAFF!" Rip shouted from the hole.

They didn't hear him. Cloudclaw and Jeweltail bounced between the room's four corners, dodging the apes' paws and clubs.

"WRAFF, WRAFF!" said Rip, jumping up and down.

Sheertooth rolled off the monkey he had knocked over and joined in as well. The tigers ran in a flowing orange figure-of-eight around the room, with the monkeys chasing after them.

Rip rolled his eyes. There was only one thing for it. He dashed forwards, jumped and sank his teeth into Cloudclaw's tail.

"WRROOOOAAAR!"

Cloudclaw jumped in the air, roaring with pain. Sheertooth and Jeweltail dodged around him. The apes, who didn't share their cat-like reflexes, stopped in their tracks and crashed into each other. Rip released Cloudclaw's tail. The tigers blinked at him, amazed to see he was still anywhere near them.

"WRAFF, WRAFF!" said Rip again. He turned around and ran through the hole.

"GRRR!" said Sheertooth, unable to believe he hadn't noticed it before.

"OOK OOK OOK!" The monkeys started scrambling back to their feet, grabbing their clubs.

Sheertooth and Jeweltail crouched low and wormed through the hole behind Rip, followed quickly by Cloudclaw.

"GRRARR!"

Just as Cloudclaw squeezed through, a grey arm shot through and grabbed his hind leg, pulling him backwards.

"Wraff, wraff!"

"OOK!"

Rip jumped forwards and bit the monkey's thumb. It released Cloudclaw and shot back through the hole instantly. The wall boomed and started to shake. Dust and stone chips fell off it – revealing writing underneath – as the monkeys pounded on it with their fists and clubs. It was starting to weaken.

"GGGRRR!"

Rip looked around. The three tigers were at the junction of the next corridor, looking back and waiting for him. Rip ran to catch up and together they raced away through the ruins.

* * *

"What the Stork is a genie bottle?" said Sari.

"It's a bottle that used to have a genie inside it," said Zara. "They use them when they can't get lamps."

"There's a genie in here?" said Zal. He had rubbed patches of dust off several of the walls around them, revealing more wishes covering each one. If every wall in the vast palace was like this, it meant the bottle was not just old, but ancient. "That's great! We can wish ourselves out."

"No, the genie's gone," said Zara, looking around at the crumbling ruins. "Long gone probably. The bottle's last owner must have used their last wish to free the genie from its curse. This palace must be the home the genie made for itself while it was here. But now it's gone, it's falling apart."

"We're inside the bottle Mr Leader was pointing at us?" said Sari. "That's the stupidest thing I've ever heard."

"OK, how do you explain the sky?" said Zal, pointing up at the strange green shade.

"If you're right, why is it crawling with giant monkeys?" said Sari.

"Genies have the power to make dreams come true," said Zara. "Now it's gone, all that's left over is the stuff it never needed to use. The magic in here is the stuff nightmares are made of. That must be why I can't use my magic."

"Why not?" said Zal.

"Most people have nightmares about things that really do scare them," said Zara. "You used to have that one where your sword broke on the night before fencing tournaments. I used to have one where I couldn't use my magic during a magic contest. Now I'm in here, it's come true."

"So you're even more useless than usual?" said Sari. "Great. How do we get out?"

"I don't know," said Zara. "I don't know if we can. Not without magic."

"Oh, Stork!" said Zal, looking around.

"Well, you two can give up if you want," said Sari. "I'm going to find my family and get out of here."

She picked up her spear and stalked away from them.

"Wait! Sari!" said Zal.

"Do not follow me!" said Sari, as she disappeared around the nearest corner.

"Oh, Stork."

"Come on," said Zara. They started to follow her, just as the wall beside them rippled.

"What the—? HOLY CAMELPAT!"

They jumped back out of the way as a giant jellyfish drifted through the wall. It was two metres tall, floating upright with a dozen long tendrils curling gently beneath its round, undulating body. It was transparent and glowing with pale blue magic. It was some sort of ghost.

"Oh, Holy Stork!"

Zara's eyes went wide with fear. She grabbed Zal's sleeve and pulled him clear of the jellyfish as it floated slowly across the corridor and disappeared through the opposite wall. Zara sighed with relief.

"What was that?" said Zal.

"A dream wraith," said Zara, as they started after Sari again. "They're really dangerous. If we see another one, stay well away from it. And above all, don't get caught inside one... Oh, camelpat!"

They rounded the corner. Another dream wraith was floating in the middle of the corridor. Sari, her eyes closed and her head nodding as she slept, was floating inside it.

"GGGGGGGGGGGRRRRRRRRRRRRRRR!!!"

Cloudclaw stood on top of a fallen column next to a broken fountain and roared as loud as he could up at the green sky. He, Sheertooth and Jeweltail listened as the roar echoed away across the ruins. No one roared back in reply.

"Wrrrrroww!" Cloudclaw whined as he jumped down.

Rip shook his head. They'd been trying to attract Sari's attention like this for ten minutes and it wasn't working. The only thing they had attracted was another pack of monkeys and several of those strange ghost jellyfish who had chased them before they had outrun them.

Jeweltail moaned and Rip watched as Sheertooth padded over and rubbed his sister's head with his own. They were missing Sari as much as he was missing Zal. But they weren't going to find them like this.

Rip lowered his nose to the sand and sniffed. The same scents flowed into his nose again: sand, dust, stone and wind, mixed with the tigers' scent of meat, claws, tails, fur and spear wax, but there was still no trace of … spear wax?

Rip paused and sniffed again carefully. This time, he detected tunic cotton, black hair and meat stew.

"Wraff, wraff!" Rip bounced up and down. The tigers looked around at him.

It was Sari's scent. He had missed it before because she also smelt so strongly of tigers. But she had been here, beside this broken old fountain not too long ago, and … he sniffed again … yes! So had Zal and Zara!

"Wraff, wraff!" said Rip again.

"Grrrrr?" said Sheertooth, cocking his head.

"Wraff, wraff!" Rip repeated.

The three tigers stared blankly at him. Rip rolled his eyes. How did humans make talking look so easy? He pushed his nose into the sand and ran about in a small, weaving circle as if he was tracking something, showing them what he meant.

"Grrrrraarrr!" said Jeweltail, her eyes lighting up as she understood. "Grrrr-arr-rarr," she said to Cloudclaw and Sheertooth.

"Grrrrr?"

"Grrrrr!"

All three turned expectantly to him. Rip shook the sand off his nose and led them forwards, following Sari's scent through the ruins.

* * *

"SARI!" shouted Zal, at the top of his voice. "SARI STORMSTRONG! WAKE UP!!!"

"Zal, stop. It's never going to work," said Zara, as Zal pushed Sari's spear into the dream wraith and prodded her with it. "It's dream magic. She'll be asleep as long as she's in there."

"What can we do?" said Zal. "Can we pull her out?"

"I don't know," said Zara. "My teachers always said to deal with dream wraiths by not going near them and breaking them apart with magic. Ugh! I don't know what else to do."

Being cut off from her magic like this was awful. It was like she was wearing thick, heavy gloves that made it impossible to feel anything properly.

"We've got to do something," said Zal, putting the spear down. "I'm going to try."

"Wait. It might not be safe."

"I've got to risk it," said Zal. "She did try to sell us to the Shadows, but we can't just leave her in there."

He plunged both hands into the dream wraith. The ghost jellyfish was thick and very sticky. Bubbles glooped between his fingers. It felt like he was pushing his hands through ice-cold glue. Zal shivered as he reached towards Sari's wrists, but before he could grab them, a powerful force gripped his elbows and drew him forwards.

"Zal!" cried Zara.

The dream wraith's tentacles rose up and wrapped around him. Zal squeezed his eyes shut and held his breath as he was pulled into its body.

Parrots cried and monkeys chattered. Insects clicked and birds chirped. Somewhere nearby, a waterfall roared into a river. Zal opened his eyes and saw green. Huge leaves grew from the branches of gigantic trees, so thick that he couldn't see the sky through them. The branches of the trees were festooned with vines and creepers and also with large, lumpy pink and yellow fruits hanging in clumps. Quakajaks. He was in the Quakajakian Rainforest.

A voice laughed somewhere below him. Zal looked down and started. He was floating upright a good ten metres above the ground, and he could see through his feet. Zal held up his hand in front of his face. His whole body had become transparent. Had he died and become a ghost?

The voice laughed again. Zal looked down properly. He was floating over a small clearing at the foot of a giant tree. Sunlight poured through the dense canopy in narrow golden beams. The clearing floor was covered in grass with giant ferns growing around its edges, and the tree's huge buttress roots arched around its base to make a shady cave.

Two full-grown tigers, a male and a female, were relaxing in the doorway of the cave, stretched out side by side with their tails wrapped around each other. In the clearing in front of them, three small cubs were rolling about on the grass. They were playing with a small, dark-haired human girl, who was wearing a torn, muddy dress and no shoes. She laughed as she hugged and tickled the cubs. They growled and purred and licked her hands and face. She was only four or five years old and there were no scars on her cheek yet, but Zal instantly recognized her as Sari.

The two adult tigers growled happily as their children and the girl played together. These had to be Sari's memories, Zal thought. The clearing was warm and quiet and peaceful.

"WOOF, WOOF! WOOF, WOOF!"

The silence was shattered as five huge brown hunting dogs burst through the undergrowth, barking and salivating. Human voices came from behind them, along with the swish of blades hacking through the bushes.

"GGGGGGGRRRRRRR!"

The adult tigers – Sari's adoptive parents – were on their feet in an instant. The father sprang into the middle of the clearing and faced the dogs, snarling and swiping with his paws to keep them at bay. The mother went to the startled cubs, picked them up by the scruffs of their necks and tossed them back into the trees roots. She picked up Sari by the collar of her dress and did the same. Then she leapt beside her mate.

"No!" shouted a voice. "No! NO!!!"

Zal looked up. Sari – the Sari he knew – was floating above him on the other side of the clearing. Somehow, she was also a ghost.

The tigers roared below them. Zal looked down. Two large nets with stone weights tied to their corners were thrown into the clearing. They landed on top of the two tigers, who immediately tried to run away and fell over, tangling their paws in the nets. The dogs danced around them, barking with triumph.

"No!" shouted Sari, hovering above them. "Not again! No!"

"Sari!" Zal shouted. "It's Zal!"

But she did not hear him. Sari was flailing in mid-air, trying to get down to the ground where she could help her family. As Zal watched, he noticed she was changing. Her body's transparency was fading and she was becoming clear and solid. Zal looked down at his own body, but it was still as transparent as a ghost. The same thing was not happening to him. And why would it be? They were inside a dream wraith. This had to be Sari's worst nightmare, or worst memory, or both, and the dream wraith was trapping her inside it.

Outside, Zara was holding on to Zal's ankles, preventing him from being pulled all the way in. She watched helplessly as Sari began to fade away inside the dream wraith as her body was drawn into her own worst nightmare.

"Zal! Hurry!" she called.

"SARI! WAKE UP!" Zal shouted, flailing around. "THIS ISN'T REAL!!!"

"No! No!" cried Sari.

Down in the clearing, a hunting party pushed its way out of the undergrowth. They were not Quakajakians, but from one of the other kingdoms, rich, well-fed men in silk robes and enormous turbans, laughing as they stood over the struggling tigers.

"No!" Sari yelled. "City-dwellers! You'll pay! You'll pay!"

Zal watched Sari's spear appear in the air next to her. She grabbed it with an almost solid hand.

"SARI!" Zal yelled. "WAKE UP!"

"GRRRAAAAARRRRRR!"

"WRAFF, WRAFF!"

Rip and Cloudclaw – not transparent, but real and solid – burst out of nowhere, sailing in mid-leap into the dream world. Cloudclaw leapt on Sari and she cried out in pain, just as Rip leapt into Zal's arms, which had suddenly become solid too. The jungle shattered like a mirror and everything went black all around it. Zal fell through the darkness, clutching on to Rip as the broken mirror shards flew past him. He could still see the clearing in them. In one, the hunting party dragged the two nets away, still laughing and congratulating each other. In another, the younger Sari crept out of the root cave, tears streaming down her face, struggling to carry all three tiger cubs at once.

Nine

"AAAAAH… *UMPH!*"

Zal landed with a thump on the sand. The air was cold and the wind was whistling between the crumbling stone walls. He was back in the palace ruins. Above him, the dream wraith shuddered. Its tentacles curled up into its body and then it broke apart in a burst of misty spray.

"Zal!" said Zara, shaking his shoulders. "Are you all right?"

"I … I…" Zal struggled to sit up. Opposite him, Sari was doing the same, surrounded by her tigers, who were mewing over her with anxious expressions. Her tunic was torn from where Cloudclaw had crashed into her. "I…"

"Wraff, wraff, wraff!"

"Rip!"

Rip jumped on to Zal's chest, licking his face. Zal hugged him, laughing with relief.

"You're fine," said Zara. "Sari?"

"CLOUD!" said Sari, sitting up properly. "SHEER! JEWEL!"

She hugged all three of them at once. They nuzzled her and rubbed her with their heads, purring. Sari looked around her.

"How… How did they…?" she said.

"Rip brought them here," said Zara. She had been very surprised to see Rip appear leading the tigers as she'd been trying to pull Zal out. "He was following your scent. When they saw you were both asleep, they jumped in to wake you up. That was what broke the sleeping spell. They reminded you of the world outside and you realized you were dreaming, so you woke up."

"But I knew I was dreaming," said Zal.

"Yes, because it wasn't your dream," said Zara.

"Wraff, wraff!" said Rip.

"But…" said Sari, blinking at Rip. "But … he helped them?"

Jeweltail purred and licked Rip's head. Rip yapped happily and licked her paw. Sari watched in astonishment.

"I saw what happened," said Zal. "To the tigers. To your family, I mean. I'm really sorry."

Sari's head shot up. Her face was furious.

"Do *not* say that!" she said, pulling the tigers close to her. "You don't know anything!"

"No," said Zal. "But I know what it feels like when someone attacks your home."

Sari stared at him.

"The Shadows did the same thing to us," said Zal. "They tried to burn down my father's shop just so we couldn't compete in the Great Race. They're trying to do it again and they've hired you to help them."

Sari was silent. The tigers purred anxiously beside her.

"What happened to you two in there?" said Zara.

"I'll explain later."

"OK, I don't know what he's talking about, but Rip just saved you," said Zara to Sari. "The Shadows trapped you in here along with us and if you want to get out and stop them, we're going to have to work together."

"Oh, on the contrary," purred another voice, "this game is about your individual wits."

The ground vanished beneath their feet.

"WHOA!"

"AAH!"

"WRAFF!"

"GGGRAARR!"

A giant hole had suddenly opened up where they were standing. Zal, Zara, Sari, Rip and the tigers dropped straight down it and landed in a tangled heap at the bottom.

"What the Stork?" Zal spat Cloudclaw's tail out of his mouth and stared up at the sides of the hole. It was twice his height, too high to jump, and the sides were simply made of loose sand. There was nothing for him to climb up.

"Magic!" gasped Zara, struggling to breathe with Jeweltail on her chest.

"You said magic didn't work here," said Sari.

"No, she said she couldn't use hers, my dear," said the purring voice. "Magic itself works just fine."

A Sphinx smiled down at them from the top of the hole. She was large and elegant, with a lioness's body and a beautiful woman's face. She was covered in golden fur and had a long tail and lots of honey-coloured curly hair that tumbled around her shoulders like a mane. She had pale crystal-blue eyes and her smile showed sharp teeth.

"Who are you?" said Zal.

"Just a Sphinx," said the Sphinx. "I'm sorry I didn't introduce myself sooner. I wanted to see if you could deal with the dream wraiths. Most of our visitors never escape from them."

"Sorry to disappoint you," said Sari.

"Oh, no! I'm delighted," said the Sphinx. "It's so rare to get people to play games with in here. It's been centuries since our last visitors."

"We don't have time to play games," said Zal. "We need to get out of here."

"I don't think she's here to help us," whispered Zara.

"Oh, no. Everyone has to play," said the Sphinx. "That's the way things work in the bottle. But don't worry. If you win, you can help yourselves."

The Sphinx flicked her tail. Thick, fast streams of sand poured into the pit from all sides, starting to fill it up.

"Camelpat!"

"Stop!"

Zal, Zara and Sari tried to scramble up the sides of the pit as the sand flowed over them, but their fingers passed straight through the loose sand walls. The tigers had the same problem. The sand poured in faster, burying their feet and rising further

"Wraff, wrugh!" said Rip, as the sand reached up to his nose.

"Now, I have a riddle for each of you," said the Sphinx, curling her tail like a question mark. "Answer it correctly if you want to live."

"All right!" said Zal, shielding his eyes from the sand. He picked up Rip before he could be buried. "We'll play!"

"Good. Then my first riddle is for you, bold swordsman," said the Sphinx. She cleared her throat. "You'll see yourself in me. But if you turn me around, you won't see anything."

"What?" said Zara.

"What's that supposed to mean?" said Sari. Even the tigers looked flummoxed.

"Are you kidding?" said Zal, as the sand reached their knees. "It's a mirror!"

"Yes!" cried the Sphinx. "Excellent!"

The walls of the pit suddenly shifted. A set of spiralling steps, also made of sand, slid out of the sides of the hole. The sand was still pouring in. Zal, Zara, Sari and the tigers scrambled straight up them, Zal carrying Rip. They clambered out just as the hole filled up completely.

The walls of the corridor shifted around them, reforming into a wide, sand-filled courtyard. The Sphinx was standing in the middle of it, with two dream wraiths floating behind her.

"Wonderful!" the Sphinx said. "You wouldn't believe how many of my guests give up without even trying. This is going to be a splendid game. Now, my second riddle is for you, my dear magician."

Six twisted, grey-brown trees with tangling branches burst out of the sand around them. In a second, they grew higher than their heads. Everyone froze in place as the branches surrounded them. The branches had no leaves, but they were covered in long, sharp thorns which stopped just centimetres from their skin.

"I am larger than any mountain, but to your eyes I am smaller than a coin," said the Sphinx. "My face is as white as snow and stained with tears of grey as I float endlessly in a waterless sea."

"A... Ummm... Let me think," said Zara.

"A fish!" said Zal. "Oww!"

The nearest branch suddenly grew an extra centimetre and pricked him with its thorns.

"No," said the Sphinx, licking her paws.

"A rock!" said Zal. "Oww!"

"No," said the Sphinx.

"A grain of sand in the Great Desert! Oww!"

"The riddle is for her," said the Sphinx.

"Wraff!" said Rip.

"No," said the Sphinx.

"WRAFF!" said Rip, as the thorns pricked him.

"A... Oww!" said Sari.

"Stop! All of you," said Zara. "It's the moon!"

"Correct!" cried the Sphinx.

The thorny branches retracted as the trees sank back down under the sand. As soon as they were gone, the walls started moving again. This time, they slid inwards. The courtyard contracted, threatening to crush them.

"My third riddle is for you, O cunning thief," said the Sphinx, leaping on top of a wall. "I am kinder than the Celestial Stork and crueller than the Cosmos Vulture. The poor have plenty of me, but the rich want for none of me. And if you eat me, you will die."

"What?" said Zara.

"A… Uh… Ummm," said Zal.

"Nothing," said Sari.

"Yes! Well done!" said the Sphinx.

"Nothing?" said Zal. "Oh, I see."

"Every thief knows that riddle," said Sari.

The walls of the courtyard slid backwards, reforming into yet another shape. The courtyard became long and narrow, and an iron gate slid into place at the far end.

"OOK OOK OOK! GAAHK GAAHK GAAHK!"

Behind the gate was another pack of apes, hooting and howling, stamping their feet and beating the gate with their clubs. The gate was slowly rising to let them through.

"Excellent! You're doing so well! You've broken my last guests' record," said the Sphinx. "They were all dead after the first two. Now, my fourth riddle is for you again, my bold young swordsman."

"What?" said Zal. "You said one for each of us!"

"I did indeed," said the Sphinx. "But I never said

how many I have in total."

"How many do you have?"

"How many grains of sand are there in the bottle?" said the Sphinx. "When you've been in here as long as I have, life gets grindingly dull. Thinking up new riddles is the best way to pass the time. Now, I am—"

"Oh, Stork!"

"Wait a minute!" said Zara. "If this is a game, why are you the only one who can ask the questions?"

"Why?" said the Sphinx, looking down at her. The rising gate paused. "Because that's the way things work here, my dear. The palace is my domain. You are my guests, so entertaining you is my duty."

"Not any more," said Zara. She stepped in front of Zal and Sari. "I want to ask you a riddle."

"Really?" said the Sphinx, looking amused.

"Yes," said Zara. "Or are you only good at making them up, not solving them?"

There was a pause. The Sphinx's eyes narrowed.

"Very well," she said. "Let me hear it."

"I always deceive, but I never lie," said Zara. "My words are real, but the truth always hides. I play a game, but make the rules, and the winner, I decide."

There was a longer pause. Zal and Sari looked at each other. Rip and the tigers frowned. Even the apes seemed to be thinking about it behind the gate. The Sphinx laughed.

"Oh, come now, my dear magician," she said. "That's cheating. You've just made up something that sounds like a riddle, but actually it isn't. A riddle has to have an answer. That is the first rule of the game."

"It does have an answer," said Zara. "You just can't solve it."

"Really?" said the Sphinx, smiling. "And what is this answer meant to be?"

"It's easy," said Zara. "You."

The Sphinx blinked. For a split second, everything was still. Then blue light flashed behind the Sphinx's eyes. She gave a cry of pain, which was half a woman's scream and half a lion's roar, then reared up, covering her face with her paws and collapsed on the sand, as part of her magic broke.

"Ha!" said Zara to the unconscious Sphinx. "I knew it! Not as clever as you think!"

"RUN!" said Zal.

Dust flew and the iron bars started to bend as the apes howled and hammered on the gate with their clubs. Zal, Zara and Rip turned away from the Sphinx and bolted down the courtyard. They skidded to a stop. The three walls joined together perfectly at the corners. There were no gaps, no holes and no doors.

"Come on!" yelled Sari, as she and the tigers ran the other way, straight towards the gate.

"What are you doing?" shouted Zal, just as the apes broke through.

Sari reached into one of her belt pouches as she ran, pulled out a small bag and ripped it open. It was filled with fine black powder, with tiny specks that gleamed like stars. Sari poured it into her palm and held her hand up before her face.

"Stay back!" she shouted. "Don't breathe in!"

Sari blew the powder out of her hand. It spread out into a wide cloud in the air as the apes charged howling straight into it. Their nostrils flared as they inhaled the powder. Their eyes widened and then dimmed. Their charge slowed to a shuffling walk, their eyelids drooped and then the apes collapsed on top of one another in sprawling, snoring heaps.

"What the Stork?" said Zal.

"Dozing dust," said Sari, holding her sleeve over

her nose and mouth and waving the rest of the cloud away. "The best sleeping powder you can buy on the black market. Come on."

They stepped over the sleeping apes, holding their noses, and ran through the twisted gate and into the apes' den. It was a wide, circular chamber with a big campfire burning in the centre. Spare clubs were resting against the round walls, in between more broken statues and dozens of small alcoves that had been hollowed out of the stone. They were filled with vases, shoes, musical instruments, writing tablets, turbans, lanterns and all sorts of other odd things all carefully displayed inside them.

"This must be their collection," said Zara.

"They collect junk?" said Sari. She picked up a spear that was leaning against the wall to replace her broken one. "That's not very... Holy Monkey!"

Piled between two of the statues was a huge mound of treasure. Gold coins were stacked up to their waists. Emeralds, rubies and diamonds gleamed in green, red and sparkling white from crowns, cups and pieces of jewellery.

"I don't think it's junk," said Zara. "I think it's what they've collected from everyone else who's

214

been trapped in here."

"Wow," said Zal. He brushed some dust off the wall and found more wishes carved underneath. "How old is this place?"

"Wraff, wraff!"

Rip had suddenly dashed over to the far side of the room and was jumping up and down beside an alcove at the wall's base. He reached in and gripped something with his teeth, trying to pull it out. Cloudclaw reached in and helped him.

"What is it, boy?" said Zal, running over to him. "Oh, yes!" He knelt down and pulled out a rolled-up carpet.

"Oh, well done, Rip!" said Zara.

"Is it one of Azamed's?" said Sari. "Can it fly?"

"Let's find out."

Zara gripped the end and pulled, unrolling the carpet. She and Zal gasped. Their mouths dropped open and they blinked at the carpet, unable to believe their eyes. It was a flying carpet – Zal had woven enough of them to recognize it instantly. It was a very old one with a simple, plain weaving pattern and rather uneven edges. But – amazingly – it was a rainbow carpet. All seven colours of magic stretched across it from one end to the other. They were dull in the dim light, but they weren't faded. Strong magic sparkled amongst the carpet pile. Inside it, Zal's weaver's hands could feel, but not see, the invisible thread, the secret ingredient which they had rediscovered in Azamed that allowed all seven colours of magic to work together and make a rainbow carpet fly.

"Holy Stork!" breathed Zara.

"Well?" said Sari, leaning over her shoulder. "Is it Azamedian?"

"No, it's not," said Zal. "It's Nygellian. It's a Forgotten Empire flying carpet. An original one!"

The carpet's pattern was a simple design. Seven snakes, each one in a different colour, wiggled from one end of the carpet to the other, and a geometric pattern ran around the four edges. Zal had seen the pattern before, carved around the doorway of the throne room in the remains of the Fire City beneath Azamed. There they had met the ancient and mad ghost of Faradeen the Eight-Hundred-and-Thirty-Fourth, the last Emperor of Nygel, who had been guarding the secret to rainbow carpets since his empire's fall. If a flying carpet from the empire's glory days was here, it meant the bottle was ancient, older even than Azamed.

"I don't know what you're talking about," said Sari, "but can it fly?"

Zara touched it with both hands. Zal did the same. For a second, nothing happened. Then the magic sparkled a little brighter. The ancient rainbow carpet rose up off the sand and floated as still and solid and perfect as their Rainbow Carpet used to.

"Thank the Stork!" said Zara.

"Great!" said Sari. "So let's go. The dozing dust isn't going to last for ever."

"Wait a minute," said Zal. "What's that?"

He had just noticed something else in the alcove where the carpet had lain. He reached in again and dragged out a large, heavy wooden chest. It was varnished and solid, reinforced with heavy iron strips. Zal lifted the lid.

"Holy Stork on a sunbeam!"

Inside it, seven large white stones rested on a red velvet lining. All of them were oval-shaped, with a glossy surface and in the dim light, they shone like moonstones.

"Zal?" said Zara.

"I don't believe it," said Zal. He closed the box's

lid. "We have to take these with us."

"What for?" said Sari, as Zal hoisted the box onto the carpet. She gestured at the treasure pile. "There's way more valuable stuff here. We can find rocks anywhere."

"They're not rocks," said Zal. "They're more valuable than all of that put together—"

"WRRAAAAAAAAAAAHHHHH!"

A sudden roar of anger interrupted him. The Sphinx bounded into the chamber, her face red with fury. A dozen apes poured through the gate behind her.

"HUMANS!!!"

"LET'S GO!" said Zal.

He jumped on to the carpet and Sheertooth and Cloudclaw bounded on behind him. Sari and Jeweltail jumped on top of the chest, and Zara scooted through into the pilot's position with Rip beside her. She pressed down with both her hands on the dusty carpet pile and the Nygellian rainbow carpet shot forwards as the Sphinx charged towards them.

"WRAAAAAHH!" The Sphinx roared again as she pounced, springing through the air as the ancient carpet zipped out from under her paws.

"Hold tight!" called Zara, as she leant backwards, tilting the carpet's front end upwards as they flew up over the chamber walls and out of the roofless palace.

"Holy Stork!" said Zal, looking over the carpet's edge. Below them the maze of rooms and corridors of the palace stretched for miles across the desert sands, dotted here and there by the orange campfires of the apes. It really had been the size of a city. The desert itself stretched even further. Zal looked ahead, trying to find the horizon. The grey sands merged into the green sky at a distance that had to be hundreds of miles away. Just how small had they been shrunk?

"Zara! Look out!" called Sari.

"Whoa!" Zal looked up and started as Zara steadied the carpet. A shiny green glass ceiling was above them. It was thick and the colours – Zal counted twenty shades of green in an instant – were so deep that they could not see anything through it. It was like they were skimming along underneath a frozen ocean.

"What now?" said Sari. "How do we get out?"

"Uh…" said Zal. From the outside, he remembered the bottle had been round. But the glass surface seemed completely flat with no curve to it, which was another sign of how small they had shrunk. They could search for years before finding the bottle's neck and even if they did, the cork was probably going to be the size of Azamed and the mountain it was built on.

"WRRRRAAAAAAAAAAAAARRGGGHH!"

The Sphinx's roar echoed up from below them. Zal felt it in his toes and in his teeth. He glanced over the edge of the carpet again. They were still above the ruins of the palace. The Sphinx was standing up on the broken dome of an observatory, her tail coiling high and her chest swelling as she roared with all her might. Then there was a rustling, screeching and squeaking sound, as if dozens of voices were speaking at once.

"Oh, monkey droppings!" said Sari. Her face had gone white.

Thousands of bats burst out of the ruins below them. Their wings sliced the air like knives as they rose up towards the carpet in vast, spiralling black clouds.

"Fly faster!" yelled Sari, flipping her spear around. The tigers leapt to their feet, almost knocking each other off the carpet. Zal drew his sword.

"Skree! Skree! Skree! Skree! Skree!"

Zara pushed down hard on the carpet, taking them to full speed, but the bats caught up with them in an instant. Their red eyes burned with rage and their small, dagger-sharp teeth gleamed as they screeched towards the carpet.

"Ha!"

"Howzat!"

"GGGGRRRR!"

"WRAFF!"

Sari drove her new spear forwards, skewering three bats at once. The tigers swiped at them with their paws and Rip bit at the flapping wings of any that came close to the carpet. Zal hacked and slashed with his scimitar and was relieved to see they were not real bats. They burst in puffs of black dust as his sword sliced through them.

Zara swerved the carpet left and right, trying to shake them off. Hundreds of bats filled the air behind them and thousands more were still rising up from the ruins, as the Sphinx's roars echoed behind them. There was no end to the glass ceiling in sight.

"Zara!" Zal shouted. "We need to get out!"

"I know!" shouted Zara. "But I don't know how!"

The screeching storm was growing by the minute.

Zal's sword muscles were burning. Sari and the tigers were panting. There was nothing but green glass and grey desert ahead of them and no way out of the bottle. Zara groaned. Even if she had her magic, what could she do in a place like this? It would take a hundred high magicians, using all of their powers together, to break through the glass. Zara looked up at the glass ceiling flowing by above them. It was just like trying to break through the wall of octopus ink staining the Rainbow Carpet. Without the seven colours to link her magic to … the seven colours?

Zara blinked. The entire ceiling was green. But inside it, she glimpsed oil-like rainbow patterns, as the light from the apes' campfires far below was reflected in the glass. Red, orange, yellow, blue, indigo and even violet swirled and rippled through the green glass. All seven colours were there. All seven colours of magic. Zara gasped.

"ZARA!" Zal shouted, slashing and jabbing at the bats. Sari was bleeding from a cut on her forehead. Jeweltail hissed as she felt a bat's razor sharp wings slice her tail. They were close enough to nip at the Nygellian rainbow carpet's tassels.

"KEEP THEM BACK!" Zara shouted.

"WHAT DO YOU THINK WE'RE DOING?" shouted Sari. "WAIT... WHAT ARE YOU DOING?" she yelled, as Zara pulled the carpet's front upwards, aiming towards the glass ceiling.

"HOLD ON!" Zara called.

The seven colours of magic were the seven elements that made up the universe. Even inside the bottle, that was still true, and she could see all seven colours in the glass. As the Sphinx had said, magic worked fine here. And Professor Maltho had said that magic was nothing more than the influence of her mind upon nature. She couldn't use her magic here, but maybe she could still use magic.

"ZARA, STOP!" yelled Zal, looking over his shoulder. "TAKE US DOWN!"

"WHAT ARE YOU DOING? WE'RE GOING TO HIT IT!" shouted Sari.

Zara closed her eyes and reached out with her mind, feeling for the seven colours in the glass. She found them instantly. The powerful, surging energy of red, the light, floating power of yellow, the violet, touching every other shade all around it, the blue, which felt like wind and water, the orange, racing like a fast river with indigo right beside it and the green, surrounding them all, lifting them up and bringing them together. The seven colours of magic that the Celestial Stork had used to make the universe were right there in front of her, where they always had been.

"ZARA!!!" shouted Zal and Sari, as they hurtled towards the glass.

Zara took hold of all seven colours. She peered through her half-closed eyes. The glass ceiling rippled open, the seven colours swirling around its edges, into a round door and the Nygellian rainbow carpet flew straight through it.

"HOLY STORK!" said Zal, his eyes wide with amazement.

All seven colours flowed past them and around them as they flew along a tunnel inside a rainbow. A few bats followed them in through the shrinking door and screeched as they disintegrated into clouds of ash. Sari gasped with wonder.

Up ahead, Zara saw another round door, this one ringed with golden light, and with the pale blue and white shades of the sky beyond it. She pressed her hands down on the soft pile and the carpet flew towards it and back into the real world.

Ten

In Shirazar it was the morning of the Champions' Race. Flags and banners flew from every spire in the city. Excited crowds were already filling the streets. Stalls and restaurants were selling out of snacks and racing breakfasts. In their guest rooms and hotels across Shirazar, the Champions of the Seventeen Kingdoms were pulling on their flying clothes, checking their equipment and preparing their means of flight. Apart from Augur Thesa and Arna Aura – who were once again running through the streets searching for their missing children – there was no sign that anything was wrong.

"Vulture's curses!" said the Leader, watching from the window of the Shadows' new hideout. "I hope

Sari Stormstrong is shivering in hell for ruining my revenge! I should have killed her as soon as she'd got us the casket!"

"We know, sir. You've been saying nothing else," said Mira.

The Shadows' new hideout was the top floor of a guest-house off Water Dragon Square. The street outside was bustling with spectators, but the Shadows were not going to be there to see the race. They were busy packing for their return to Azamed.

"Don't be impertinent, Mira," said the Leader. "My perfect revenge was ruined. Yes, we got them in the bottle, but I never got to see the look of horror on their faces when they realized they hadn't defeated me. Now I never will."

"Could we possibly let them out again, sir?" said Etan, looking at the bottle, which was standing on one of the shelves.

"Don't be ridiculous. They're probably already dead," said the Leader. "No. I'll just have to settle for taking revenge on Azamed. But it won't be as satisfying."

"OK. But are you sure setting the Knife Demon on the Champions wouldn't help?" said Etan. "I think it's getting restless."

The stone box rocked from side to side on the table in the centre of the room. It shook its way along the table's edge, knocking over two scrolls and a pot of pencils.

"Be patient!" said the Leader, rapping on the box with his knuckles. "No, there's no point. We saw at the carpet shop that it's enchanted only to attack flying carpets. It'll have to wait until we're back in Azamed."

"But Denjar's is not the only carpet shop here, sir," said Hara. "We could take it for some exercise before we go. It would be a good parting compliment to the Shirazans."

"An excellent idea," said the Leader.

TIIIIIIIIINNG!!!

On the shelf, the genie bottle shattered into green dust. The Nygellian rainbow carpet, back to its normal size and overloaded with Zal, Zara, Rip, Sari and the tigers, burst out of it.

"HOLY VULTURE!" yelled the Leader.

Hara and Mira's swords leapt out of their scabbards. Zal's sword was already out. Sari's spearhead sang as it clashed against Mira's blade as Zara landed the carpet on top of the table, knocking the Knife

227

Demon's box to the floor. It landed lid down, trapping the Knife Demon inside it.

"GET THEM!" shouted the Leader, reaching for his own dagger. "AARGH!"

Rip leapt off the carpet and sank his teeth into the Leader's wrist before he could draw his dagger. Cloudclaw was right behind him and pinned the Leader to the floor as Etan struggled to load his crossbow.

"HA!" Sari knocked Mira's sword aside. Mira staggered backwards and fell over Jeweltail who had slipped around behind her. Zal's sword clashed as he fenced with Hara until Sheertooth grabbed her ankle in his teeth and pulled her off balance. The Knife Demon rattled furiously in its box as it sensed another carpet. Zara grabbed the largest, heaviest book on the shelf and dropped it on top of the box.

"TAKE THAT!" yelled Etan, firing his crossbow at Zara. She ducked underneath the arrow and it sank into the wall. She rolled sideways and called up her magic. The rainbow fire of all seven colours blazed into life inside her again. Blue magic surged down her arms and filled her hands and she batted Etan's second arrow aside, before shooting back a violet stun spell.

"YAAAAAHH!!!" yelled Etan, flying backwards as the spell hit his chest like a hammer. He bounced off the wall and landed on the floor in a heap. Sheertooth stamped on his crossbow, breaking it in half. Zara sighed with relief that her magic was back.

"Now, Sari!" shouted Zal.

"Hold your breath!"

Zara breathed in and then held her nose. Rip and Cloudclaw scurried off the Leader as Sari blew her second bag of dozing dust over all four Shadows. They stopped struggling to stand up and collapsed on the floor.

"Well done," panted Zal, as the Shadows started snoring.

"Don't mention it," said Sari, picking up her spear. "Being betrayed by a client is bad for business. It encourages my other clients to do the same thing if I don't do something about it."

Zara quickly knelt by the Knife Demon's box and turned it over. The Knife Demon clattered wildly inside it, but the lid stayed closed.

"What are we going to do with that?" said Zal. "Can you break the spell?"

"I don't know how," said Zara, lifting the box

up. "We'd better give it to Professor Maltho. If the Academy had the Crystal Flowers of Kandara, they should be able to deal with this."

"OK, but keep it closed," said Zal, as Zara placed the box on the Nygellian rainbow carpet. "This carpet is our last chance to be in the race."

"No, it isn't," said Zara. "We don't need this carpet any more. We can race on the Rainbow Carpet. Our Rainbow Carpet."

"What?" said Zal.

"Where is your Rainbow Carpet anyway?" said Sari.

"We left it at Miles' house," said Zal, eyeing the box. "OK. We've got two days until the race—"

"Wraff, wraff!"

Rip was standing beside one of the scrolls that had fallen off the table in the commotion. He nudged it with his nose, making it unroll. It was a copy of *The Shirazar Star*.

"What's wrong, boy?" said Zal, picking it up. "What's... OH, CAMELPAT!"

"What is it?" said Zara.

"The date!" said Zal, pointing to it.

He dropped the scroll onto the table and ran to

the window, stepping over the snoring Leader. He threw it open and looked out onto Water Dragon Square. The Shirazan flag was flying from the roof of the Royal Palace in the distance. Under the shade of the square's orange trees, people were excitedly making bets. Others were hurrying out of the square in the direction of Plateau's Edge Street and the other good places to watch the race.

"Oh, no!"

"We must have been inside the bottle longer than it felt," said Zara. "We've lost two whole days!"

"What time does the race start?" said Sari.

"Midday."

"Then you've got about one hour," said Sari, looking up at the sun.

"Oh, thank the Stork! Then we're OK," said Zara. "I've still got time to fix the Rainbow Carpet."

"ZAL! ZARA!" cried Miles, as he opened the door. "Where have you been? Oh, Holy Stork! Sari Stormstrong!"

"Nice to meet you too," said Sari, pushing past him into the house. "Did we really have to bring them?"

231

"Yes, we did. They're wanted in Azamed," said Zal, steering the Nygellian carpet through the door with the still-sleeping Shadows piled on top of it. "Don't worry, Miles. She's here to help."

"Sorry to barge in," said Zara, "but we need the Rainbow Carpet."

Fluffy mewed sharply at Rip, just as he led the tigers in. Fluffy took one look at them and jumped into Miles' arms.

"Let's make this clear, Thesa. I'm not helping you," said Sari. "I'm settling the score with my ex-client. You're helping me."

"Your ex-client?" said Miles, trembling.

"Yes. We found them," said Zal, pointing to the Shadows. "Sorry it's been two days. We were trapped in a bottle."

"Oh! The Shadow Society!" said Miles. He leant against the wall as Zal landed the Nygellian carpet in the corner of the room. "You caught them! What a relief! But… Oh, great! You found another rainbow carpet!"

"Yes, but don't worry about the race rules," said Zara. "We're not going to need it any more."

The Rainbow Carpet – their Rainbow Carpet –

was standing in the corner of the room. Zara went straight over to it and unfurled it. The black and grey mess of the ink stains rolled out across the floor. But the carpet's colours, the seven colours of magic, were still there beneath the ink, just as they were in everything else in the universe. Zara placed both her hands on the weaving and summoned up her magic. It came quickly, still warm from her duel with Etan. Zara closed her eyes and reached through her memories. She felt the carpet pile beneath her palms and remembered what the carpet was like when it was new and perfect. She pictured the seven bands of colour and how they flowed and merged together. She pictured the carpet's decorations – the coiling water dragons, the flying doves and the ancient Nygellian crown – just as she had first seen them when the carpet hung newly finished on Zal's spare weaving frame. Zara opened her mind, her magic and her heart and reached into the Rainbow Carpet.

The carpet shivered. Magic sparkled through the black and grey. The carpet rose up off the floor, slowly and shakily, and then it steadied. The dried ink cracked, revealing the seven colours like the sun breaking through clouds. The ink fell off in a shower of black dust and the Rainbow Carpet floated perfect and pristine again.

Zara sighed.

"Thank the Stork!" said Zal.

"That was amazing," said Miles.

"We're back in the race," said Zara.

"Congratulations," said Miles. "What a relief. Two rainbow carpets. And I take it that's the Knife Demon?"

Fluffy sniffed at the box. The Knife Demon rattled again.

"I don't understand," said Sari. "If this is your carpet, what happened to it?"

"The Shadows used the Crystal Flowers of Kandara on us," said Zara.

"They did?" said Sari. "How did they get hold of them?"

"What do you mean 'how'?" said Zara. "You stole them for them."

"Never mind that. We need to celebrate," said Zal. "Does Celeste still drink that great pomegranate and mango juice?"

"Oh, of course," said Miles. "She always wants it before the race. I'll get some."

"Don't worry. I remember where you keep it."

"What are you talking about?" said Sari. "I stole the Knife Demon for Mr Leader. The Crystal Flowers were for my other client."

"What other client?" said Zara.

"No! Wait, Zal! I can get it!" said Miles, as Zal strode into the kitchen.

"Don't worry, I remember," said Zal, as he went through the kitchen door. "Second shelf on the right next to the…"

Zal froze in place. Standing on the kitchen table was a vase of yellow and violet flowers. The stems, leaves and blossoms were carved out of solid crystal, exactly as they had been drawn in Professor Maltho's book. Next to them was a clear glass decanter, shaped like waves in a stormy sea, filled with a liquid of constantly shifting shades of blue. Beside it was a neatly folded pile of shimmering silver cloth, which looked as fine as silk. Beside that there was also an elegantly curved silver hunting bow, strung with a bowstring as thin as spider's web. A wooden box sat open beside it, with a set of dark red chess pieces inside. There was also the handle of an elegant scimitar, the metal carved into the shape of roaring flames, and a flat metal boomerang with razor-sharp edges, carved all over with air-flow channels. Zal's expression changed as, one by one, he recognized all the items illustrated in *The Shirazar Star*. Everything that had been stolen in the crime wave was laid out and neatly organized on the Nocturnes' kitchen table.

"Camelpat," said Miles, behind him.

Zal's neck prickled like lightning. He spun around, grabbing his sword hilt and wrenching it from his scabbard just as Miles moved, like a striking cobra, drawing his sword in the fastest diagonal-draw-cut Zal had ever seen. His friend's eyes had turned to stone.

SHHINNNG!

Their blades met in mid-air. Zal's scimitar snapped, one inch above the hilt. The broken steel blade flew across the kitchen and stuck, quivering, into the wall. Miles' free hand shot forwards, clenched into a fist, and ploughed into Zal's nose, sending him stumbling backwards.

"ZAL!" shouted Zara.

Zara, Sari, Rip and the tigers had come running as they heard the swords being drawn. Sari raised her spear and red magic filled Zara's hands, just as Miles pulled out a small, bulging black pouch and held it out towards them, holding his nose with his other hand. He squeezed and the pouch burst in a cloud of dozing dust.

Sleep fell over Zal, enveloping him like a warm blanket. He was suddenly so tired that holding his eyes open felt like pushing against a stone weight. The floorboards rushed up towards his face as darkness fell.

"Still slow, Zal," he heard Miles say. "Always too slow."

Zara groaned as she woke up. Her head felt like it was filled with fog and she had to force her eyes to open. There were two more groans beside her, as Zal and Sari woke up.

"Hi, guys," said Miles, who was crouching on the floor, just finishing tying Cloudclaw's legs together. "I'm sorry."

Zara tried to lift her hand to rub her eyes, but ropes bit into her wrists. She, Zal and Sari were tied back to back in three chairs in the middle of the living room. Across from them, the Shadows were tied to the sofa, slumped against the ropes and still snoring. The tigers were lying tied up on the floor, and Miles had even tied Rip to Fluffy's cat basket. Miles' own fast six-colour carpet, which Augur and Zal had given to him as a birthday present years ago, was floating by the door, loaded with the stolen items and ready to go.

"MILES!" said Zal, as he woke up properly. He struggled against the ropes, rocking his chair. "It was you! You total camelpat! It was you all the time!"

"I'm so sorry," said Miles. "I know that doesn't really cover it, but I am. I never dreamed it would get this bad."

"You stork dropping! You used the Crystal Flowers on us."

"That was an accident," said Miles. "I was figuring out how they worked. What were the chances that you would be flying over the park at the same time?"

"Let me out of this chair! I'm going to—"

"You're my other client?" said Sari, flexing her arms against the ropes. "No wonder you always wore that hood and the false beard."

"Yes, that was me, and thanks for all your help," said Miles. "You were better than I ever hoped for. You got me everything."

"Grrr? GRAAARRR!"

Cloudclaw woke and found himself tied up. Miles jumped out of the way just in time as he thrashed on the floor, waking up Sheertooth and Jeweltail. Their muscles bulged as they strained to break the ropes.

"You're planning to sabotage the Champions' Race?" said Zara.

"I wish I wasn't," said Miles. "Believe me. But I've got no other choice. I tried everything I could think of to persuade Dad not to compete this year, but none of it worked. This is the only option I've got left."

"Have you gone crazy?" said Zal, still struggling. "He's the Red Squirrel! Why the Stork wouldn't you want him to compete?"

"Because he's getting too old for it," said Miles. "He and Celeste both are. They can't fly like they did when they were young any more. But Dad's set on winning this year and I don't want him to get hurt."

"So you're going to ruin the race to stop them?" said Zal.

"No, of course not!" said Miles. "I'm going to make sure he wins."

He shook his head sadly.

"You don't know Dad as well as you think you do. You don't know how important being the Champion of Champions is to him. It's his life's work. If he loses now, in his last race, it could destroy him."

"You're going to help him?" said Zara.

"Exactly," said Miles. "I hope I won't have to. Dad might still win on his own. I'm just going to be there to make sure he doesn't lose."

Miles stood and pushed his sword into his sash. He went over to his carpet and quickly counted the stolen items again, checking they were all there. Zara looked around and sighed with relief. Miles had put the Knife Demon's box on a shelf, well away from the two rainbow carpets.

"What about us?" said Zara. "We know your plan now."

"Don't worry. You're not going to remember it," said Miles.

"I've got a very good memory," said Zal.

"After Dad's won the race, I'm going to come straight back here and feed you all some amnesia potion," said Miles. "I got it from the same magician who sold me the dozing dust. Then I'm going to set everything up so it looks like you captured the Shadow Society – and its hired thief, Sari Stormstrong – but sadly you breathed in some dozing dust during the fight and slept through the race. You missed your chance to be Champions, but you'll still get to be heroes."

"But Miles, think for a minute," said Zara. "What if your dad finds out it was you? That's going to hurt him more than losing."

"He'll never know," said Miles, opening the door and sitting down on his carpet. "All I need to do is get him through this race so he can retire happy and then everything will be OK."

"But Miles!"

"I'm really sorry."

Miles pressed down with both hands and the six-shader glided neatly through the door, loaded with magical weapons. Miles reached back and pulled the door shut behind him.

"Rip!" Zal called. "Wake up, boy! Chew through the ropes!"

"Don't bother," said Sari, standing up. The ropes fell loose around her chair.

"How did you…?"

"I'm the greatest thief in the Great Desert," said Sari. "You don't get to my level without knowing all there is to know about knots."

She knelt down beside Jeweltail and freed her with a single pull on the ropes.

"We've got to stop him," said Zara. "Sari, untie us. We'll pay you."

"Don't worry, that won't be necessary. I'm coming with you anyway," said Sari, as she freed Sheertooth and Cloudclaw. Cloud went straight over to Fluffy's basket and started chewing Rip free. Rip groaned as he woke up.

"You are?" said Zara.

"I've just been betrayed by two clients in a row," said Sari. "I have to deal with this now. I've got my reputation to protect."

She reached between Zal and Zara's chairs and pulled and the ropes around their wrists instantly loosened.

"Uuurgh?" came a voice from across the room. "What's happening…?"

They looked around as the Leader raised his head. Hara, Mira and Etan were stirring too.

"Oh, I'd forgotten about you," said Zara.

"Vulture's curses!" said the Leader, sitting up and struggling against his ropes. "Where are we? How did you get out of the bottle? How are you still breathing?"

"Your plan was stupid," said Zal.

"We'll tell you about it later," said Zara, "after the Royal Protectors get here."

"What? No! Don't you dare summon them!" said the Leader. "I'll curse you with every enchantment in the book! I'll make you die a thousand deaths, ten thousand painful deaths and a hundred thousand … agonizing deaths!"

"Just be quiet," said Zara. She quickly went to the Rainbow Carpet and checked it was OK. "You can sit there until we get back. Come on, we need to go. We've got half an hour until the race."

"Wait, I just need to get something," said Zal. He hurried over to the wall where Miles' spare swords were hanging. He lifted one down that was roughly the same size and shape as his own broken one.

"Good idea," said Sari, picking up her spear as Rip and the tigers climbed onto the carpet.

"Yes. I can't believe he broke mine," said Zal, as he tucked the sword into his sash and tried drawing

it. "Mistress Shen never taught me how to do that...
Whoa!"

The sword leapt up out of the scabbard and
almost shot out of his hand. Zal had only pulled
gently, but there had been no resistance, as if the
scabbard wasn't holding the blade at all.

"What the...?" Zal pulled the scabbard out of his
sash and peered down it. He held it under his nose
and sniffed. "Butter...? BUTTER! MILES! YOU
STORK DROPPING!"

"Butter?" said Zara.

"It's lined with butter!" said Zal, holding up
the scabbard. "Diagonal-draw-cuts! That's how he
always wins!"

"Cheating's something he's good at," said Sari.

"Come on. Let's go," said Zara.

"That total camelpat! I'm going to kill him!" said
Zal, as the Rainbow Carpet glided out of the door.

Above the starting line, the flags of all Seventeen
Kingdoms fluttered from the Arch of Champions.
The arch was made of snow-white marble and
carved all over with the story of Emperor Clearju
and the first Champions' Race. It stood on the very

edge of the plateau, looking out over the desert and the first section of the race track.

Behind it was a great open courtyard that served as the starting area. A dozen servants were dusting and polishing the Royal Pavilion ready for the Empress's arrival. On a raised platform, the ten judges were taking their places behind a long curved table, that was laid out with maps, rule books and score sheets. The gates had just been opened and the Royal Protectors were letting in the spectators, some of whom had slept in the street all night to be sure of getting good seats. In the crowds, people were placing bets, praying to the gods and casting good-luck spells for their kingdom's Champions. In front of the Royal Pavilion, Paradim Nocturne was standing with a group of friends, including Augur and Arna, Professor Maltho and Mistress Shen.

"It's so good to see you two again!" said Paradim, shaking both their hands at once. "You don't come to Shirazar often enough. It's been far too long!"

"Yes, but you never come to Azamed either," said Arna, shaking his hand and glancing over his shoulder.

"Thank you, Paradim. How's Celeste?" said Augur,

anxiously searching the crowd.

"Oh, raring to go," said Paradim. He was a tall and strong man, with a weathered, but handsome face. His hair was already brushed and combed back into his famous long red ponytail, though it was now streaked with a couple of strands of grey. "I felt her feathers trembling when I gave her breakfast this morning. But where the Stork are Zal and Zara?"

"Nowhere!" said Augur.

"They'll be here!" said Arna. "Don't worry. They'll both be here. On time. I hope."

"Ah, off for a last-minute training flight, are they?" said Professor Maltho. "So they fixed the Rainbow Carpet? I knew Zara could do it. Your daughter has the potential to become a very fine high magician one day, Arna."

"Great potential is also the way I would describe your son's swordsmanship," said Mistress Shen to Augur. "Assuming he learns to use his brain before it gets him killed, that is."

"A training flight? Oh, that must be where Miles is," said Paradim. "He's been really distracted for the last three days. So tell me, just how fast is one of these rainbow carpets?"

"Ummm…"

"Dad! Mr Aura!"

"ZAL!"

Spectators and Royal Protectors jumped out of the way as the Rainbow Carpet came through the crowd with Zal, Zara, Rip, Sari and the tigers onboard. Augur and Arna ran to meet them. Zal sighed with relief to see the Royal Pavilion was empty. The race could not start without the Empress.

"Where have you two been?" said Augur. "Do you know how worried we were?"

"Yes, it was like the night before the Great Race all over again!" said Arna. "I was almost expecting to hear you'd been found hurt! Or dead! What have you been doing?"

"I'm sorry," said Zal. "We don't have time to explain."

"Oh, also like last time?" said Arna.

"Who is this?" said Augur, pointing at Sari and the tigers.

"This is Sari. She's a friend."

"Hello," said Sari.

"Zal! Where have you been hiding?" cried Paradim, arriving behind their fathers. "And Zara!

We finally get to meet!"

"Thank you, Mr Nocturne. It's an honour to meet you," said Zara, shaking his hand. "Sorry, Dad. It's a long story."

"Yes, very long. Is Miles here yet?" said Zal.

"No, we thought he was coming with you," said Paradim.

"No, he … he said he was going on ahead," said Zal.

"Oh, maybe he stopped to feed Fluffy," said Paradim. "But still! Here we all are at last!"

"We are?" said Zara.

"I always knew this day would come," said Paradim. "Zal was born to be a racer, and anyone who can enchant the perfect flying carpet must be too. I knew I'd have to fly against you both eventually. And I can't think of a better day for it."

At that moment, several trumpets sounded. Clapping echoed across the courtyard as the Empress – wearing a dress made of pure-white swan feathers – arrived on the Royal Pavilion with her ministers. A bell rang and a race official shouted for all the Champions to make their way to the starting line.

248

"Right! This is it!" said Paradim, rubbing his hands together. "I'll see you all at the finishing line. Hopefully, right behind me."

He strode off and disappeared through the gates into the contestants' area.

"Let's go," said Sari.

"You're coming with us?" said Zara.

"I already said I was. I can't settle things with my ex-client from here," said Sari.

"OK, but they're going to have to stay here," said Zal, nodding to Sheertooth, Cloudclaw and Jeweltail.

"What?" said Sari. Sheer, Cloud and Jewel pressed up against her. "No way! Not a chance."

"The rules are that Champions can only have one passenger with them," said Zara. "We can take you or one of them, but not all four. Then how do you get even with Miles?"

"You're bringing Rip."

"He's one of the Champions of Azamed," said Zal. The Caliph had officially given Rip the title as well for all the times he had helped Zal and Zara during the Great Race.

Sari hesitated. Then she sighed. She knelt down

249

and put her arms around the tigers' heads, pulling them close to her face. She whispered to them for a moment, and Jeweltail whimpered with surprise. Cloudclaw whined, but Sheertooth growled deep and short. All three tigers nodded.

"They'll stay," said Sari, standing up. "But you have to keep an eye on them," she said to Augur and Arna. "Don't let them run off or eat too much."

"Us?" said Augur.

"Keep an eye on them?" said Arna, stepping back.

"You'll be fine," said Zara, as the race official gave the final call. "Come on. Let's go!"

Inside the contestants' area, the Champions of the Seventeen Kingdoms were assembled together for the first time. All the means of flight in the Great Desert were lined up side by side and excitement filled the air.

At the head of the crowd was Prince Neeaj, Champion of Pursolon, sitting in his flying throne. It was an enormous, solid wood chair, decorated with gold leaf and carved with pictures of Pursolon's heroes. Magic glowed in the runes carved into its legs and across its base as the throne floated a foot above the ground, bobbing gently in the air. Next to him, and scowling at him, was his great rival, Elsai Wavewind, the Champion of Caldyn, sitting on the neck of her roc. Like Paradim, she had raised the giant, brown-feathered bird of prey since it had hatched. Before the Champions' Race, she had ridden her bird against Prince Neeaj in many local races, where they had always drawn. Each of them was hoping that, this time, they could beat the other.

Beside them, Mara Hazela, Champion of Skandia, was brushing the twigs of her broomstick. It was made from wood from the evergreen forests of her northern kingdom and Mara had enchanted it herself. She wore the distinctive black pointed hat of a Skandian witch that she had enchanted so it wouldn't blow off in the wind once she was flying. Next to her sat a giant, green-scaled Heaven Steppe dragon, coiling its tail on the ground and blowing smoke from its nostrils. The Champions of the Heaven Steppe – a three-man family team from the Rock Slope Clan, were adjusting their harnesses and feeding the dragon last-minute energy-boosting snacks. Beside them, the Champions of the Silk

Lands – a four-man family team – had just finished assembling their large and beautiful silk box-kite. It was made of orange silk and though it flew mostly by wind magic, they had deliberately chosen the spot beside the dragon to use the hot air it breathed to give them an extra push over the starting line.

On the other side of them were the Heaven Steppe team's great rivals, the Champions of Frostbite, another three-man team, preparing their giant, white-scaled snow dragon, which breathed icy mist where the other breathed smoke. The race organizers had made sure to put the Silk Lands team in between them to keep them from fighting before the race even started.

Next to them were a line of individual Champions. Jula Rua, the Champion of Endsali, was sitting on his large, grey-feathered gryphon, chatting to Akaha Naktep, the Champion of Hothath, who was riding his lamassu, a magnificent winged lion with a golden mane and silver wings. Beside them was Laya Ursula, the Champion of Xalam, grooming the gleaming wings of her white pegasus, and then the Champions of Katrasca – a seven-man family team – who were sitting on a giant floating plate that was rotating slowly in the air on the starting line. They were determined to break their record of being the Champions who crashed every single year.

Beside them was a giant glass water tank, holding two huge, silver-scaled flying fish. The Champions of the Emerald Archipelago, the dark-haired twin sisters, Fan and Lan Xuan, were swimming like fish in the tank with them. Hoto Hibari, the Champion of Yamaroto was beside them, using a large umbrella to keep any splashes away from his elegant origami crane. Folded from a single giant sheet of paper, the model bird was large enough to ride on and Hoto had folded and enchanted it himself. Next to him were Max Rafatar, the Champion of Tabaras, riding a giant phoenix with rainbow tail feathers, and the Champions of Quakajak, a huge nine-man family team from the Gemstone tribe, positioned along the length of the long green body of their giant-winged jungle serpent. Beside them were the Champions of Gothopar, a five-man family team, were preparing the rigging on their vimana, a small, elegant sailing ship, which was tethered to the ground by a large anchor, its hull and sails enchanted with flying magic. Finally, in the very middle, was Paradim

Nocturne, the Champion of Shirazar, sitting astride his giant stork Celeste, who stretched her wings, wider than both the dragons, and cawed at the golden sun.

Zal stared at the other Champions as he, Zara, Rip and Sari hurried to the last remaining space. This was not like racing at home at all. The Rainbow Carpet was tiny compared to the other means of flight. The other contestants just glanced at them as they glided up to the starting line. Many of them had flown in the Champions' Race for years and had only been beaten by Paradim Nocturne.

"Can you see Miles?" whispered Zara.

"No," said Zal.

"He won't be here," said Sari, pulling off the scarf she had tied over her hair and around the sides of her face to hide her scars in case the Royal Protector at the gates recognized her. She nodded through the arch towards the desert. "He'll be out there waiting for us, using the Mirror Curtain as an invisibility cloak. That's what I'd do."

"Oh, great," said Zal. "Now how do we stop him?"

"We'll just have to find a way," said Zara.

The bell rang again, signalling to the Champions

that it was time. Everyone inched forward, right up to the starting line. Applause flowed across the courtyard as the Empress stood up on the Royal Pavilion and drew out a red silk handkerchief, the same one Emperor Clearju had used to start the first Champions' Race five hundred years ago. He had only meant to blow his nose, but a gust of wind had blown the handkerchief out of his hand across the starting line and everyone thought it was the signal. Silence fell as the Empress held the handkerchief up and then released it. The crowds and the contestants breathed out as they watched it fall and land softly on the courtyard stones. With a roar of cheering, the Champions leapt across the starting line.

Eleven

The Katrascan team crashed straight into the top of the Arch of Champions, breaking the nose off a carving of Emperor Clearju.

"Every single year," said the Empress, shaking her head, as the other Champions dodged the falling shards of crockery and burst out through the arch and over the desert.

The ground fell away beneath the contestants as they passed over the edge of the plateau. Instantly they were high in the air, hundreds of metres above the sands. Zal, Zara and Sari held on tight as wind buffeted the carpet from all directions. Zal held Rip under one arm and gripped the carpet with the other. Around them, the other contestants were all flying at least as fast as the Rainbow Carpet. Now he understood why Azamed hadn't won the Champions' Race in two hundred years!

The first stage of the race was simple. They followed a long curve, marked by red flags on the dunes, to take the Champions clear of the city and allow them to warm up. As Shirazar fell behind them, the flying became easier. The Champions spread out through the open air, finding space to fly properly. The Rainbow Carpet steadied and Zal set Rip down behind Zara.

"Any sign of Miles?" called Zara, over the wind.

"Of course not! He'll be invisible!" shouted Sari. "But he'll be here somewhere!"

Zal scanned the desert around them. The Rainbow Carpet was in the middle of the field, with the other Champions flapping and soaring and gliding all around them. Paradim was close to the front on Celeste, but Akaha Naktep on his lamassu was in the lead.

Zara's neck prickled. She felt the magic inside her core stirring as she sensed magic being formed close by. The red, orange, yellow, green, blue, indigo and violet shades were all moving and mixing, combining in blazing, glaring, pure white magic.

"Something's happening!"

"Where?"

"ROOOOAAAARRRR!"

The lamassu roared with pain. It bucked in the air, almost throwing Akaha off, as a white flash like a small, thin shooting star flew out of nowhere and cut it across its front leg. The winged lion slowed, trying to lick its injured paw and fly at the same time. Akaha leant forwards to see the wound and then sat up in his saddle. He held out both arms, crossed them across his chest and threw them out again. He was withdrawing to treat his lamassu's injury.

Paradim pressed forward on Celeste to take the lead. But Jula Rua was right behind him, and his Endsali cliff-gryphon was young and strong. Zal watched as the distance between them closed fast.

"CAAAAWWWW!"

The gryphon suddenly dropped from the air. Another white flash had streaked across the sky, cutting through its left wing. Jula Rua held on, shouting encouragement to his gryphon as it descended, flapping hard and made an awkward, tumbling landing in the sand dunes.

"What's happening?" said Zal.

"It's Miles!" said Sari. "He's using the Moon Bow!"

"The fourth thing you stole for him?"

"Yes. It shoots arrows made of moonlight!"

That was why they couldn't see them. Moonlight was invisible in daylight. Zara had learnt years ago how, even though it looked white or silver or both, the light of the moon contained all seven shades of magic, mixed together more perfectly than any magician could ever hope to achieve. Rip yelped as another white flash shot past the carpet. The other Champions had realized something was going on. They slowed down, looking around, and more white flashes streaked around them.

"What do we do?"

"Hang on," said Sari, feeling in her belt pouches. "I can deal with this."

She pulled out a large, jagged crystal which was as clear to look through as glass and started rubbing it against her sleeve.

"Is that a sun crystal?" said Zara, looking over her shoulder.

"Don't look straight at it!" said Sari.

259

Zara quickly turned to face forwards again. The sun crystal glowed behind her, growing into a burning white blaze. Zal shielded his eyes. Rip flopped his ears over his. The other Champions around them tried to look at it, but it was so bright that they quickly had to look away. Sari held the crystal up above her head, letting its light shine out all around them.

"There they are!"

Zara cautiously squinted. The light made the gold and blue of the desert and the sky clearer and brighter than before, and now she could see the arrows, cutting silver lines as they streaked through the air. Of course! Moonlight was invisible during the day, but it was made of all seven colours mixed together. Sari's sun crystal contained enough yellow and orange magic that it acted like a magnet; pulling the yellow and orange shades out of the arrows, breaking up the moonlight mixture and making the arrows visible.

"Yes!" shouted Zal. "Oh, Stork! Look out!"

The Champions veered left and right to avoid the arrows. The Heaven Steppe dragon and the Quakajak serpent tried to bite several of them. Sari and Zal held on as Zara wove the carpet through the silver streaks.

The Champions were looking around, trying to see who was holding the bow. Zara glimpsed expressions changing as they realized what was happening. Someone else had been shooting at them.

The arrows stopped. The air was clear again as the Champions reached the end of the starting curve and began the first long leg over the desert around the city. Paradim was still in the lead.

"Why's Miles stopped?" said Zal.

"He doesn't want to give himself away," said Sari. "We could work out where he is by following where the arrows are coming from."

"Following where the…?" said Zal. "Wait. I've got an idea. Zara! Take us higher."

"Why?"

"Just do it!"

Zara leaned backwards and the carpet rose. They climbed high into the air, well above the other Champions. Zal peered over the carpet's edge. The midday sun was shining brightly and the flying Champions' shadows were cast clearly on the dunes below. Zal counted the lizard wings of the dragons, the bird wings of Celeste and the roc, the rippling ribbon of the Quakajak serpent and all the others, including the small black rectangle of the Rainbow Carpet. And there, up ahead and to the left, was the small shadow of another flying carpet.

"Over there!"

The Mirror Curtain could make Miles' carpet invisible, but it couldn't hide its shadow. Miles was out in front of them, probably flying backwards to keep pace with the race and have a good view of everything.

"Oh, well done!" said Zara, as she saw the shadow.

Zal stared at the shadows on the sands and then at the positions of the Champions in the air. His swordsman's brain quickly calculated the angles and distances, figuring out where Miles had to be.

"There! He's over there!"

Zara turned the carpet in the direction Zal was pointing. Zal kept one eye on the shadow in case Miles tried to move. Sari picked up her spear and Rip growled as the two shadows on the sand grew closer together.

A tiny flame suddenly appeared in the air ahead of them. Orange and red fire burned in thin air around the space where Miles' carpet was. Zal blinked as they flew straight towards it. The other Champions stared too. Suddenly, the flame roared and blazed like an angry beast and stretched out sideways, forming a gigantic sword blade made entirely out of fire.

"HOLY STORK!"

Rip barked with astonishment. Zal and Sari threw themselves flat on the carpet and Zara ducked as the giant blade, four metres wide and almost a mile long, swept over their heads. The sun was blocked out by the orange flames, mixed with blazing red magic, like a swordsmith's forge. The skin on the back of their necks burned and the air turned hotter than an oven as it passed them.

"It's the Fire Scimitar!" gasped Sari. "He actually got it to work! It's meant to be broken!"

"He's always been good with swords!" said Zal.

The fire blade swept out horizontally above the sand dunes, as if it had been drawn from a giant invisible scabbard in a horizontal-draw-cut. It was so huge that Miles couldn't change its direction quickly and most of the Champions flew up over the top or zipped under it, but two of them were not fast enough. The Silk Lands' spinning box-kite flew too close to the blade and one of its sides burst into flames from the heat. Hoto Hibari steered his origami crane up and over the fire blade, but the paper singed and crumpled. The box-kite started to fall and the origami bird went after it.

"ZARA!"

"Hang on!" shouted Zara. She swung the carpet around and they dived after the falling kite. Zara summoned her blue and indigo shades, the colours of water magic. She threw out her arm, steering the carpet one-handed, and a fluffy white cloud formed in the air ahead of them. The cloud burst open and thick, heavy rain started pouring from it, showering down over the box-kite. The flames hissed out in seconds. Unfortunately, the water made the kite fall even faster.

"Oh, Stork!" said Zara.

"Wait!"

The Silk Lands team climbed expertly around the sides of their damaged kite and used their weight to flip it over, holding on to the burnt side. The other three sides filled with air like a parachute and the Champions of the Silk Lands waved in thanks as the kite drifted slowly down towards the dunes.

"Zara! Quick!" called Zal.

Zara looked up and saw the origami bird plummeting towards the desert. Magic glowed as Hoto Hibari tried to repair the damage. Zara steered the Rainbow Carpet after it, pushing her rain cloud ahead. They weren't going to make it in time.

"HHHHHSSSSSSSSSS!"

The snow dragon from Frostbite swept over their heads, leaving shivering cold air in its wake. It dived down after the origami bird and blew a long stream of icy mist from its jaws, enveloping the paper crane. The flames went out instantly. Hoto Hibari, covered in frost and shivering, signalled he was OK and steered down for a safe crash landing in the dunes.

"That's five down already," said Sari. "He … WHOA!"

The Fire Scimitar's blade swept back over their heads. Zara only just moved the carpet out of the way in time. Rip yelped and jumped away from the back edge as the tassels were scorched.

"Don't worry. I've got an idea," said Zara, as her rain-cloud followed them. "We need the snow dragon! HEY! FROSTBITE! THIS WAY!"

The Frostbite team's captain saw Zara's signal. He waved back. The Rainbow Carpet and the snow dragon flew up in a loop and turned around back in

"Oh, great!" said Sari, picking up her spear. "The Demon Chessmen!"

The objects started to grow. Zal watched with amazement as the small chess pieces expanded into stone statues, three metres high. Behind their stone helmets, red magic blazed in their eyes. Their stone muscles flexed as they hefted giant stone swords, axes and shields, ready to do battle with the Champions.

"Hold tight!" said Zara, as the first Chessman reached them.

Zal ducked as the Chessman swung its sword at them. Sari knocked the blade aside with her spear and jabbed the statue in the eye. Rip barked furiously at it and Zal drew his sword.

Swords clashed up and down the gorge. The Emerald Archipelago twins fired arrows from their short flying bows. Poison darts from the Quakajak team's blowpipes studded the Chessmen's shields. The larger flying animals roared, bit and clawed at the statues. The Heaven Steppe dragon breathed fire over two of them, reducing them to molten lava. There was a boom as the small bronze cannons on the Gothopar team's vimana fired and blasted several of the Chessmen to smithereens. Mara Hazela spiralled past on her broomstick, hurling combat spells at the Chessmen behind. Zara joined in, but her magic burst against their red stone shields.

Zal blocked swords and parried axe blows as the Demon Chessmen tried to cut the Rainbow Carpet with their weapons. The statues were strong and their blows ripped at his arm muscles. To make matters worse, there was no way to strike back. Their stone armour, carved straight out of their stone bodies, would blunt his sword before it did any damage. It was like fighting the Knife Demon all over again. Sari gasped beside him, having the same problem.

Zara fired another spell and watched it burst against a Chessman's breastplate. It was flying so close that the magic almost blew backwards into her face. Rip barked furiously at it and tried to bite its foot. It was no use. The Chessmen were enchanted to protect them from spells, and they were flying so close that... Flying so close?

"Zal! Sari! Hold on!" Zara shouted. She put both hands on the carpet and veered them sideways straight towards the Chessman.

"What are you doing?" Sari screamed.

"Zara! Stop!"

"Hold on!"

"Wraff!

The Chessman flew backwards as the carpet flew towards it, keeping the space between them so it could swing its axe. Zara flew so close to the canyon wall that the carpet was almost touching it. The Chessman raised its axe and was smashed to pieces a second later as it flew backwards into a rocky outcrop.

"YES!" cried Zal.

The other Champions saw what Zara was doing and quickly copied her. The Xuan sisters flew in a spiral, luring three Chessmen after them before they flew through a hole worn by water in the canyon side and the statues crashed into the edges of it. Prince Neeaj made his throne dive suddenly and two more Chessmen smashed into each other trying to follow him. The Quakajak serpent wrapped its tail around one of them and bashed it against the canyon wall, breaking it in half. The Heaven Steppe dragon and the vimana's cannons took care of the final two, just as they reached the end of the canyon and climbed back over the desert.

"ZAL! ZARA!"

They looked up. Flying down from above them came a large yellow sofa. Zal recognized it from Professor Maltho's study. The Professor and Mistress Shen were riding on it.

"I take it I was right!" said the Professor, as he steered the sofa, which had been made in Pursolon from the same wood as Prince Neeaj's throne, alongside the Rainbow Carpet. "Someone is trying to sabotage the race!"

"I'm afraid so," said Zara.

"Never fear. We're here to help," said Mistress Shen. "Professor! Can't this thing go any faster? I've already missed my chance to match blades with the Demon Chessmen."

"I'm doing my best. It wasn't made for racing," said the Professor.

"Don't worry. He's got plenty of stuff left," said Sari. "The Vessel of Tears, the Crystal Flowers and the—"

"LOOK OUT!"

ZZZZZZIIIIIIIINNNNNNGGGGGGGG!

They all ducked as a spinning triangle of metal flew through the air just above their heads. It was as large as a clothes hanger, with a smaller triangle

271

cut out of its centre to help it fly. Its surface was polished like a mirror and its straight edges were as sharp as a scimitar blade.

"And the Boomerang of Astigor," said Sari.

"Splendid!" said Mistress Shen.

She leapt to her feet on the sofa, drawing both her scimitars as the spinning boomerang flew in a wide circle back towards them. It was the personal weapon of Astigor, the ancient Shirazan hero, who was remembered in songs and legends across the Seventeen Kingdoms for his heroic deeds against the Forgotten Empire. Mistress Shen spun on her toes, her hair and scarlet robe flying and her scimitars spinning about her like a whirlwind, hitting the boomerang as it closed on them and knocking it away from the carpet.

"Well done, my teacher!" said Zal.

"Don't toady, Thesa," said Mistress Shen. "But it is a good feeling. It is too long since I truly tested my blades!"

Right at that moment, the boomerang changed direction. It flashed across the desert towards the other Champions, who were just catching up. Moving faster than the Demon Chessmen, the Boomerang flew down on the Gothopar team's vimana.

"Oh, Sparrow Gods!" said Mistress Shen.

The Boomerang spun, cutting-edges first, through the vimana's rigging, sending ropes and sails flying free.

"Oh, Great Celestial Elephants!" cried the team captain, spinning the sky ship's wheel desperately as it plunged down towards the desert. The crew managed to balance it out by rushing to the back end and it ploughed softly into the nearest dune.

"Quickly, Professor! After it!" shouted Mistress Shen.

The Boomerang spun towards Mara Hazela, who dived out of its path and zig-zagged her broomstick low between the sand dunes, trying to shake it off. But it caught up with her quickly and sliced through the bristles at the end of her broomstick. Mara plummeted downwards and landed in a dune in a cloud of sand.

"Oh, camelpat!" said Zal, as the Boomerang flew back up and headed straight for Prince Neeaj.

The Prince was ready for it. Drawing his scimitar, he stood up on the seat of his throne and parried the Boomerang aside. Steering his throne with just his feet, the Prince held the Boomerang off, slashing and cutting to keep it at bay. But in the end, it was too fast for him. Distracting the Prince with a vertical spin, it flew up over his head and down the other side of the throne. Before he could turn around, it cut through all four of the throne's legs in a shower of sawdust.

"Oh, Merciful Ancestors!" shouted the Prince

The throne dropped like a stone. The Prince lost his footing and fell after it, plunging down towards certain death.

"CAAAAAWWWW!!!"

In a streak of brown feathers, Elsai Wavewind's roc flew down in a steep dive and caught the Prince in its talons. It flapped upwards, carrying the Prince by his shoulders as his throne smashed to pieces far below.

"Miss Wavewind?" said the Prince in disbelief. "Elsai?"

"You're not dying today, your royal pain-in-the-backsideness!" Elsai Wavewind shouted, as the Prince climbed up the roc's feathers behind her. "We've got unfinished business!"

The Professor's sofa caught up with the Boomerang. Mistress Shen's swords sent it spinning sideways again. It righted itself, and then spun straight back towards the Rainbow Carpet.

"Oh, Stork!"

Zal drew his sword and knocked the Boomerang aside as it reached them. It flew around in a small circle and came straight back at the carpet. Sari leant over Zal's shoulder and knocked it backwards with the point of her spear. Zara threw another spell as it came in a third time, but her magic bounced off the polished metal.

"Wraff, wraff!" said Rip.

"Not now, Rip!" said Zal, slashing the Boomerang away from the carpet's corners. The Professor's sofa was hurtling back towards them, trying to catch up.

"WRAFF, WRAFF!"

"Wha—?"

SHHIIINNNNNNNNGGGGG!

A black streak flew in out of nowhere, striking the Boomerang and sending it spinning sideways, twenty feet away from the carpet. The black streak slowed down enough for them to see it, and its forked blade.

"OH, CAMELPAT!"

Zal's mouth dropped open as he recognized the Knife Demon. He looked down. There were now three carpet shadows on the sand dunes below them. The new one was speeding towards them, moving as fast as the Rainbow Carpet. He looked up as the Nygellian rainbow carpet approached, ridden by the four Shadows.

"HA, HA!" cried the Leader. "VENGEANCE IS MINE! GET THEM, DEMON!"

Zal and Sari turned back to the Knife Demon, raising their weapons. The Knife Demon turned in a circle and shot straight towards them, aiming its points at the centre of the Rainbow Carpet, just as the Boomerang spun in and knocked it off course.

"What the Vulture?" said the Leader.

The Knife Demon spun end over points, confused, as the Boomerang flew after it and hit it again. The Knife Demon recovered quickly and flew back at the Boomerang. Steel rang against steel as they collided.

"What are you doing, you stupid thing?" shouted the Leader. "Not that! Get the carpet!"

"I don't think it's listening, sir!" said Etan, who was flying the Nygellian Carpet.

The Knife Demon and the Boomerang circled and then attacked each other again. Sparks flew as the

276

two enchanted weapons fought a vicious dog fight in mid-air. The Knife Demon thrust with its points and cut with both its edges. The Boomerang spun around to pound the Knife Demon with its corners.

"Let's get out of here!" said Sari.

"Good idea!"

Just as Zara pushed the carpet forwards, the Knife Demon struck. It was heavier than the Boomerang and made of thicker metal. It hit the Boomerang with its pommel, knocking it sideways. As the Boomerang tried to recover, the Knife Demon flipped over and drove its points straight through the Boomerang's thin metal, until all that showed was its hilt. Zara felt a crack like a mirror breaking as the Boomerang's magic was broken. The Knife Demon, with the bent and crumpled Boomerang speared on it, turned towards the Rainbow Carpet.

"Oh, Stork!"

"Thesa! Retreat!" shouted Mistress Shen, behind them.

"Ha, ha! Yes!" said the Leader. "About time!"

"WWWRRRROOOAAARRR!"

Fire burst across the sky as the Heaven Steppe dragon caught up with them. It breathed a stream of orange flames that washed over the Knife Demon as it dived towards the Rainbow Carpet. The flames faded, revealing the Knife Demon and the Boomerang melted together into a glowing lump of molten metal. Red hot drops of liquid steel dripped from it as it wobbled in the air, flying at half its previous speed.

"Vulture's curses!" shouted the Leader, punching the air and accidentally hitting Etan.

"NOW!" shouted the captain of the Heaven Steppe team, over his shoulder.

"HHHHSSSSSSSSS!"

The Heaven Steppe dragon pulled away and the snow dragon flew down into its place. Guided by the Frostbite team, it opened its jaws and breathed another cloud of ice mist over the Knife Demon, which was struggling to fly in a straight line. As the mist cleared, the Knife Demon rocked in the air, cooled solid into its new shape. Cracks appeared in the metal from the sudden change from hot to cold as Zara steered the Rainbow Carpet past it. Behind them, the two dragons flew around in a circle and then approached the Knife Demon again, flying side by side.

"TIME IT RIGHT!"

"DON'T MISS!" the two team captains shouted at each other.

They closed in and the two dragons peeled apart, flying around the Knife Demon on opposite sides. Both dragons swung their tails – which ended in large, heavy triangles of bone – and smashed them against the Knife Demon, hitting it from both sides at once. The melted mess of the ultimate anti-flying carpet weapon broke apart into a hundred shards of metal. They fell down towards the dunes like rain. Zara felt another crack, this one like a mountain falling, as the Knife Demon's magic was sucked away into the winds of time.

"NOOOOOOOOOOOOOOO!!!" shouted the Leader, falling to his knees.

"HURRAH!" yelled Professor Maltho.

"Curses!" said Mistress Shen.

"THANK YOU!" shouted Zal, as the two dragons spiralled above them.

The desert flattened out as they approached the final part of the circuit around Shirazar. Suddenly, several yellow and violet flower petals spun through the air around them.

"Oh, not again!"

"The Crystal Flowers?" said Sari.

"Don't worry. Leave this to me," said Zara. "Zal! Find Miles."

"STAY BACK!" Zal shouted and waved to the other Champions, except for Paradim, who was in the lead again. He searched the sand dunes beneath them for Miles' carpet shadow.

The flower petals brushed the carpet's edge and drifted away glowing with magic just like last time. Zara placed her hands on the carpet and reached out into the flower petals, finding the magic again. The flower petals faded, almost to nothing, as she drew the stolen magic back out of them and poured it straight back into the carpet. The Rainbow Carpet's colours shimmered, but didn't fade, and it stayed steady and solid in the air.

"Over there!" said Zal, as he found the right shadow.

"Got it!" said Zara. She steered the carpet towards where Zal was pointing and reached into her pocket.

She steered them through the storm of petals, focusing on the point above the horizon where Miles had to be. The stream of petals grew narrower and narrower as they followed it backwards towards its starting point.

"There it is!" said Zal, as they saw the point where the flower petals were appearing out of thin air.

Zara pulled Etan's spell-suppression talisman out of her pocket, where it had been since they had escaped the bottle. She couldn't see Miles, who was still hidden by the Mirror Curtain, but the petals were visible. As they glided over the spot the petals were coming from, she threw the talisman. The chain spread out in the air as it fell and then disappeared. The flower petals vanished as well, as the talisman landed over the vase of Crystal Flowers. They heard a vague curse from an invisible voice, and then the *whoosh* of a carpet moving away.

"Yes! Take that, Miles!" shouted Zal. "Come on. This is the last leg!"

They were now flying over Pinnacle Plain. The desert was almost flat, but tall, sharp rocks rose like daggers out of the ground at irregular intervals. The Champions began weaving through them as they entered the final stage of the race, flying back towards Shirazar. Zara slipped into the pilot's place and pressed down with both hands, pushing the carpet faster. They were in second place with only Paradim ahead and they were finally catching up.

"We can do it," breathed Zal. "We can win!"

Suddenly, the sky darkened. Zal, Zara and Sari looked up as black storm clouds appeared out of nowhere and blocked out the blue sky. Lightning crackled and thunder rumbled. The clouds rolled and twisted and rain started pouring down in sheets across the Great Desert.

"Holy Stork!" said Zal. Zara threw up one hand and green magic streamed from her palm, forming into a large green umbrella to keep the carpet and its passengers dry.

"It's his last weapon!" said Sari, as the rain hammered on the umbrella. "The Vessel of Tears!"

Zal nodded. He had read the description in the news scroll. The glass vessel contained a liquid that was said to be the tears of one of the Celestial Stork's children, the Stork of Storms. No one knew if it was true, but what was certain was that if you opened the vessel and poured out even a small amount of the liquid, an instant thunder and lightning storm would appear.

The other Champions shouted, cried and cursed

behind them. The pegasus from Xalam, the phoenix from Tabaras, the roc bearing Elsai Wavewind and Prince Neeaj, and the Quakajak team on their serpent all struggled to stay airborne as their animals' wings got waterlogged. Professor Maltho was desperately trying to squeeze water out of the sofa's cushions. One by one, they went down to land in the wet sand dunes between the rocky pinnacles. Paradim stared back in disbelief from first place – he could not understand how the rain was missing Celeste.

"We've got to stop him!" called Zal.

"Don't worry!" said Zara. "It's still a sunny day!"

The storm clouds could not change that. The midday summer desert sun was still there, shining brightly behind them. The sunlight was filled with the yellow shade. Zara focused on the yellow stripe in the carpet between her feet, and on the yellow magic inside her. She reached up with her mind, searching for the same feeling beyond the twisting clouds. It was very easy to find now that she knew how.

Sunlight burst through the clouds in a giant gold and yellow beam. The rain pattered to a stop. The thunder died and the storm clouds dissipated and faded away, revealing the blue sky again. Zal's clothes started drying as the sun's heat reached them, just as Shirazar came into view on the horizon.

"Where's Miles now?" said Sari, looking around.

"Why? That was his last weapon, wasn't it?" said Zal.

"Yes, so he'll be getting desperate," said Sari.

"Don't worry," said Zal. He stood up and checked his new sword in its scabbard. The butter made drawing it so much easier, though it couldn't be good for the blade. "I'll take care of him."

"How?" said Zara.

"Just trust me," said Zal, and jumped off the carpet.

The wind rushed through his hair and ripped at his tunic. He heard Rip howl and Zara and Sari shout behind him as he plummeted straight downwards. The sand dunes hurtled up towards him and he started to think he might just have made a terrible mistake before...

"UMMPH!"

Zal landed flat on his face on thin air. He was lying on a transparent, solid surface, like a sheet of glass, watching the desert dunes flow by beneath him. His hands were touching a smooth, filmy material, with soft carpet pile underneath.

"Meeoww!" said Fluffy, her fur standing up on end.

"You idiot!" said Miles, from the pilot's place. "What the Stork were you thinking?"

"I knew you wouldn't let me die," said Zal. "We've been friends for too long."

He stood up, carefully testing the invisible surface beneath his feet. Miles had draped the Mirror Curtain over his carpet and somehow, by standing on it, they were also invisible. So too were the Moon Bow, the hilt of the Fire Scimitar and the vase of Crystal Flowers, with the spell-suppression talisman tangled up between their stalks, which were all sitting on it.

"Oh. Good guess," said Miles. He placed his hand on his sword hilt. "Now we're going low. You can jump off into the dunes."

"Not a chance," said Zal. His placed his hand on his own sword.

"Zal, I won't let you die, but that doesn't mean I won't hurt you," said Miles.

"Likewise," said Zal. He spread his feet apart and flexed his knees.

"Don't bother," said Miles. "We both know I'm faster. I've beaten you enough times."

"Has that one got butter in the scabbard as well?" said Zal, nodding at Miles' sword.

"Camelpat!" said Miles, as he noticed Zal was wearing one of his spares. "That's just to give me an extra edge. I don't *need* it to be faster."

"Let's find out," said Zal.

They faced each other. Miles paused for a second, and then drew. It was the fastest Zal had ever seen, faster than any of their previous competitions, faster than when he had broken Zal's sword. He didn't even see Miles' arm muscles move. One moment Miles' sword was in his scabbard and one half-second later, it was flying through the air towards Zal's neck. Zal let go of his sword and ducked underneath it.

"WHOA!" said Miles. The blade sailed over Zal's head and the speed of his swing pulled Miles off balance. Zal grabbed Miles' legs by the knees, lifted and threw him over the edge of the carpet with a wrestling throw that they had practised together hundreds of times in the sawdust pits at the School of Swords.

"YAAAAAAHHH ... OOMPH!" Miles yelled as he fell ten feet and plunged head first into a sand dune.

"MEEOOOWWWW!" shouted Fluffy, and dived off the carpet after him. In seconds, the speeding six-colour carpet had left them far behind.

"Too fast, Miles," said Zal. "Always too fast."

Zal pulled the Mirror Curtain off the carpet and let it blow away on the wind behind him. Pushing the Crystal Flowers, the Fire Scimitar and the Moon Bow overboard, he sat down in the pilot's place. He leant backwards and steered the carpet up high into the sky. Zara slowed the Rainbow Carpet down so he could catch up and Zal jumped across, letting Miles' carpet fall away. He landed on the Rainbow Carpet as the white marble of the Arch of Champions came into view.

"Nice work," said Sari, as Rip barked with joy and licked Zal's face.

"Never mind that! This is it!" said Zara, pushing the carpet to full speed.

There were five contestants left in the race. The two dragons, the Xuan twins and Paradim and Celeste were accelerating towards the finish. Paradim was still in the lead, his red ponytail flying behind him. As Zara pushed the carpet, they started catching up. The flying fish and the snow dragon slipped behind them. The distance closed between the carpet and Celeste's tail feathers. Paradim looked back and saw that they were catching up. He smiled with excitement and turned forwards to urge Celeste on. Rip barked with excitement as they gained on him.

"This is it!" breathed Zara. "We're going to win—"

"NOT SO FAST!"

The Nygellian rainbow carpet suddenly arrived next to them. Zal rolled over, drawing his scimitar, and Sari swung her spear, fending off Hara and Mira as they swung their swords at the Rainbow Carpet. Zal blocked the Leader's dagger and Etan fired his crossbow at Zara, which she blocked with her magic.

"AAARGH! VULTURE!" screamed the Leader, as Rip bit his wrist. "TAKE THEIR CARPET DOWN!"

Paradim looked back again at the sound of swords clashing behind him. Sparks were flying as Zal and Sari furiously fought with Hara and Mira. The two female Shadows were superbly trained to fight together, blocking and counter-attacking for each other. Zal tried to keep fighting and get through their defences as his arm muscles started to burn.

There didn't seem to be any way to beat them, unless…

"TALLY-HO!"

Paradim and Celeste, who had turned around and flown in a circle away from the finishing line, came in behind the Shadows' carpet.

"HOLY VULTURE!" screamed Etan. "STORK!"

"Take that!" yelled Paradim, as Celeste reached her long neck forward and bit through the Shadows' carpet. Her spear-length beak almost sheared it in half. The Nygellian carpet folded instantly. Hara, Mira and Etan fell into the middle and the Leader – deciding he wanted to live more than he cared about his followers – leapt across to safety on the Rainbow Carpet.

"SIR!"

"AAARGH!"

Rip sank his teeth into the Leader's ankle as he landed. The Leader kicked him off and spun around to face Zal, Zara and Sari, pulling out his spare dagger.

Zal moved by reflex, without thinking. He whipped his sword out in a perfect diagonal-draw-cut, as fast and precise as any Miles had ever performed, hitting the Leader's dagger and sending it flying from his hand. Sari flipped her spear around and hit the Leader between the eyes with the end of the shaft. His eyes rolled back as he collapsed unconscious. Zal and Sari grabbed him before he could fall overboard, just as the Rainbow Carpet shot, in first place, across the finishing line.

Twelve

The spectators' seats erupted with cheering. Shouts and applause rang out all around the Arch of Champions as Zara landed the Rainbow Carpet back in the middle of the courtyard. The spectators from Azamed and all the other kingdoms were on their feet clapping, having enjoyed every minute of the race.

"We did it!" cried Zal.

"Wraff, wraff!" barked Rip.

The wind washed over them from Celeste's wings as she arrived and landed behind them in second place. Paradim jumped down from his saddle and dashed over to them. To their surprise, he was smiling.

"Ha, ha! Well done!" he cried, shaking all their

hands. "I knew it! I knew it all along! If anyone was going to beat us, it would be you two!"

"Thanks, Mr Nocturne," said Zal. Celeste leant over them, cawing happily. Rip yapped back and Zal rubbed her beak.

"Miles was right," said Paradim. "Twenty times was too many. But I'm still glad I did it. That was the most exciting Champions' Race I've ever flown in."

"It certainly was," said Empress Haju, who had just arrived with two of her ministers and her bodyguards. "But who on earth were those lunatics on the other carpet?"

Paradim bowed and Zal and Zara jumped to their feet. Sari nodded politely.

"It's a long story, Your Majesty," said Zara.

"ZAL! ZARA!"

Augur and Arna rushed out of the crowd, surrounded by Sheertooth, Cloudclaw and Jeweltail, who jumped into Sari's arms at once and knocked her over.

"YOU DID IT! YOU DID IT! I KNEW YOU COULD!" cried Arna, hugging both of them. "Sorry, Paradim."

"Don't worry about it," said Paradim. "I wouldn't be happy to lose to anyone else."

"Oh, second place is perfectly respectable, Paradim," said the Empress. "Especially after you turned back to save these two and … and who is your friend?"

"Oh. Umm…" said Zal, looking at Sari and the tigers. "This is…"

"Shara Strongstorm of Kandara, Your Majesty," said Sari, bowing to the Empress. The tigers lowered their heads as well. "Please forgive Sheer, Cloud and Jewel. My family runs a tiger reserve. Zal used to train with me at the School of Spears and as soon as he told me what was going on, I insisted on coming along to help."

Behind them, the other Champions started to arrive. The Xuan twins flew their flying fish straight back into their water tank with a big splash, showering the snow dragon and the Heaven Steppe dragon as they landed side by side. Their teams leapt down from their saddles to congratulate one another. Behind them, the sofa landed with the Professor and Mistress Shen on board, followed by two five-colour magic carpets, carrying several Royal Protectors and

Hara, Mira and Etan, who were all in handcuffs.

"Uuuuuhhh?" The Leader regained consciousness and sat up on the Rainbow Carpet. "Etan? What happened?"

"I was about to ask you that," said the Empress. "Who are you and why were you trying to ruin my first Champions' Race?"

The Leader paused as he realized where he was, and then leapt off the carpet to make a run for it. He stopped dead as the tigers cornered him, growling.

"Uh... Not a chance, Your Empressness! Forget it!" he said, as her bodyguards grabbed his arms and handcuffed him. "I'll tell you nothing. I swear, by both of the Cosmos Vulture's nostrils, you'll get not one single word out of me! Isn't that right, my friends?"

Hara, Mira and Etan all scowled at him, remembering how he had left them to die and leapt to safety on the Rainbow Carpet. They had only survived because the Royal Protectors' carpets caught them as they fell.

"Miles?" said Paradim.

Zal and Zara looked around. Another five-colour carpet had just landed. Miles and Fluffy, covered in sand, were on board with two Royal Protectors.

"Miles! What the Stork were you doing out there?" said Paradim, running over to him. "And where have you been?"

"Dad," said Miles, looking terrified. "I—"

"He was helping us," said Zal, quickly stepping over to them. "Thanks a lot, Miles. You were great. Though you could have been a bit quicker when they were using the Fire Scimitar on us."

"Yes!" said Zara. "And what happened to you being able to fight all the Demon Chessmen with one hand tied behind your back? And great job saving us from the Boomerang of Astigor."

"And we'll be discussing you testing out the dozing dust on Sheer, Cloud and Jewel later," said Sari.

"What?" said Miles. "I... I..."

"We found out what the Shadows were planning three days ago," said Zara, to Paradim and the Empress. "I put an invisibility spell on Miles's carpet so he could fly with us to help out when we needed it. We just hadn't counted on them using the Mirror Curtain to be invisible as well."

Miles stared at them in amazement, blinking sand out of his eyes.

"WHAT?" said the Leader. "That's not what happened! Not at all! It was—"

"Sir!" said Etan. "You just swore to the Cosmos Vulture not to tell them anything!"

The Leader stuttered to a stop. His face froze as he realized he could not speak without breaking his vow. His eyes shot to Hara, Mira and Etan, whose angry expressions showed they were in no hurry to speak the truth either.

"Who are you?" said the Empress.

"I can answer that, Your Majesty!" said Lord Dasat. The Azamedian Ambassador skidded through the crowd, red faced and puffing. "They're members of the Shadow Society. They're all wanted for a long list of crimes back in Azamed."

"Good. We'll add them to the charges," said the First Minister of Shirazar. "Along with sabotaging the Champions' Race. Arrest them all, Protector."

"Miles! I'm so proud!" said Paradim, hugging his son. "So that was why you didn't want me to race this year! No wonder you were so distracted!"

"But ... but Dad," said Miles, "you came second. You ... you lost!"

"Oh, that doesn't matter," said Paradim. "I've

won more times than my fair share. You were right. I am getting too old for this and I've been Champion of Champions long enough. It's someone else's turn. And I can't think of anyone better."

"You still could have won if you hadn't turned around," said Zal.

"No, you would have overtaken me anyway," said Paradim. "I know the winds of the race well enough to tell that. And what kind of Champion would I be if I'd won by leaving you at their mercy?"

"Nobly spoken, Paradim," said the Empress.

"Three cheers for the new Champions!" called a man in the crowd. "Hip Hip!"

"HOORAY!!!" the spectators shouted. Rip barked and the tigers roared and even Sari clapped as Zal and Zara were hugged and congratulated. Then she tapped Zal on the shoulder.

"I'd better be going," she said, under the cover of the second cheer.

"What? Why?" said Zal.

Sari nodded through the crowd. Captain Curta was pushing through the spectators towards them, staring fixedly at Sari. In his hand was a WANTED poster.

"Oh, Stork!"

"Don't worry. You can thank me later," said Sari. She beckoned to the tigers. "Come on, Sheer. Cloud. Jewel. Let's go."

"Wait, Sari," said Zara, but she vanished into the crowd as the Azamedian spectators crowded around to congratulate their Champions.

The official award ceremony took place four hours later in the throne room of the Royal Palace. Under its great domed ceiling, Zal and Zara stood on the marble floor before the throne. Their fathers and friends, the other Champions, and all the important ministers and dignitaries in Shirazar watched from seats around the edges as Paradim picked up the trophy from a golden stand and passed it over to them, recognizing them as the new Champions of the Great Desert.

"Congratulations to you both," he said. "It feels like there was never any doubt it would be you two."

"Thank you," said Zara, as Zal took the trophy.

"You've certainly earned it," said the Empress, from the throne.

"Hurrah!" cried Arna. He and Augur led Miles,

Mistress Shen, Professor Maltho and the rest of the crowd in cheering.

"The only sad thing is that this is the last year you'll be racing, Paradim," said the Empress. She sighed. "The last time anyone born in Shirazar will be racing."

"Well, yes. But we always knew I wouldn't last for ever, Your Majesty," said Paradim. "And who knows? I found Celeste. Maybe someday, some other Shirazan will find a new means of flight…"

"Actually," said Zal. "They won't need to."

Paradim and the Empress looked at him.

"We won't?"

"You've already got one," said Zal. "Mr Aura…"

"Yes, yes! I have it right here," said Arna. He stepped out of the crowd, carrying the ancient wooden chest that Zal had found inside the genie bottle. "What is this? It's really heavy."

"Zal?" said Paradim.

Arna set the box down on the floor and Zal knelt down to open it. Paradim gasped as he saw the seven large white ovals inside.

"I thought you'd recognize them," said Zal. "I've heard the story enough times that I did."

"I don't believe it!" said Paradim. He knelt down, wide-eyed and ran his hands over the ovals. "The eggs!"

"Eggs?" said the Empress.

"Yes, Your Majesty. The same kind that Celeste hatched from!"

All the Shirazans in the throne room gasped. The Empress stood up from her throne. Excited talking ran through the crowd. Professor Maltho dashed forward to examine them.

"They're old, but they've been preserved by magic," said Zal. "They should be able to hatch. And if they do, you'll have seven new storks for the next Champions' Race. And if they breed…"

"By the Stork's wings!" said Paradim. "This is wonderful! This isn't the end of Shirazans flying! It's the beginning!"

"You're right," said Professor Maltho, holding one up. "Though why haven't they hatched already? The spell on them has been broken. It should be more than warm enough."

"Perhaps they are in the wrong place," said Mistress Shen. "The Sparrow Gods have created many kinds of birds that fly all over the world, but return to their own homelands to lay their eggs. Perhaps they need to be—"

"Back at Stork Lake," said Paradim. "Very well. It seems I'm going on one more journey to get a means of flight for Shirazar."

"Wait, Dad! No. Forget it," said Miles, running forward. "You said an hour ago you were getting too old for the race. You're definitely too old to be going all the way to Frostbite again."

"I agree," said Zal. "It's a long, hard, difficult and dangerous journey. It has to be someone young, brave and unafraid of danger. Miles, you'll have to go."

"What... Me?" said Miles. Then he noticed Zal and Zara's expressions. "Oh. Yes. Definitely. I'll go."

"But Miles! You hate cold weather," said Paradim.

"Yes, but I ... nearly failed to stop the Shadows ruining the race," said Miles. "Someone has to go. You're right, Zal. It should be me. You have to stay here, Dad."

"Someone's going to have to teach the riders for the new storks," said Zal.

"I suppose you're right," said Paradim. He placed his arm around his son's shoulders. "Very well,

Miles. You've ridden on Celeste enough times and she knows the way to the lake. Take her and the eggs with my blessing."

"And mine too," said the Empress. She turned to Zal. "This is splendid news. How can we ever repay you?"

"You can start with the prize money, Your Majesty," said Arna. "We've lost a considerable investment in rainbow carpets thanks to the Shadows and that accursed Knife Demon."

"Of course," said the Empress, smiling. "Bring it in, Minister."

"Yes, Your Majesty," said the Second Minister, going out through the throne room's double doors.

"You needn't worry about the Knife Demon, by the way," said Professor Maltho. "I examined the pieces. The enchantment is broken completely. There's no way it's coming back."

"A pity," said Mistress Shen. "It would have been a worthy foe to test my swords against."

The throne room doors were suddenly thrown open and banged against the wall as the Second Minister skidded back in, looking shocked.

"Your Majesty!" he said. "It's gone!"

"What?" said the Empress.

"The chest with the prize money!" said the Second Minister. "It's been stolen!"

"WHAT?!" said Arna.

"Someone used a feather to pick the lock on the window!" said the Second Minister, as Captain Curta ran out to investigate. "The room's empty. They took everything: the chest, Miles Nocturne's flying carpet and everything that was stolen in the crime wave. The only things left in the room are some orange fur and a few tiger footprints!"

"Sari!" cried Zal and Zara together.

"Who?" said Professor Maltho.

"We'll explain later," said Zal. "Miles?"

"Yes. I'm coming," said Miles, checking his sword.

"Good. This is your fault, after all," whispered Zara, under her breath.

"You're the ones who teamed up with her," Miles whispered back.

"Who is Sari?" said the Empress, as Zal, Zara and Miles ran out of the throne room, with Rip and Fluffy leading the way, to fetch the Rainbow Carpet.

* * *

303

Out over the Great Desert, the last few butter-flies fell behind Miles' carpet as it flew away from Shirazar.

Sari counted the last of the twenty thousand gold pieces prize money and closed the lid of the chest. She leant back against it and scratched Jeweltail's head. Zal and Zara would get over it. They were going to be famous all over again, and they would soon be rich from selling their rainbow carpets. Mr Leader and his idiots would soon be in prison and when the Shirazans found where she had hidden all the stuff she had stolen for Miles Nocturne – in his bedroom – her score with him would be settled as well. He might have turned out to be good-hearted in the end, but she was the greatest thief in the Great Desert. She had her reputation to consider.

Sari turned the carpet towards the sunset and flew forwards towards her next job and her next adventure.